FREE GIFTS FROM
THE ARMADA COLLECTORS' CLUB

Look out for these tokens in your favourite Armada series! All you need to do to receive a special FREE GIFT is collect 6 tokens in the same series and send them off to the address below with a postcard marked with your name and address including postcode. Start collecting today!

Send your tokens to:

Armada Collectors' Club
HarperCollins Children's Books,
77 - 85 Fulham Palace Road,
London, W6 8JB

Or if you live in New Zealand to:

Armada Collectors' Club
HarperCollins Publishers Ltd.
31 View Road, Glenfield,
PO Box 1, Auckland

THIS OFFER APPLIES TO RESIDENTS OF THE U.K., EIRE AND NEW ZEALAND ONLY.

1 TOKEN

CS

The Chalet School series by Elinor M. Brent-Dyer

1 The School at the Chalet
2 Jo of the Chalet School
3 The Princess of the Chalet School
4 The Head Girl of the Chalet School
5 Rivals of the Chalet School
6 Eustacia of the Chalet School
7 The Chalet School and Jo
8 The Chalet School in Camp
9 Exploits of the Chalet Girls
10 The Chalet School and the Lintons
11 A Rebel at the Chalet School
12 The New House at the Chalet School
13 Jo Returns to the Chalet School
14 The New Chalet School
15 A United Chalet School
16 The Chalet School in Exile
17 The Chalet School at War
18 The Highland Twins at the Chalet School
19 Lavender Leigh at the Chalet School
20 Gay Lambert at the Chalet School
21 Jo to the Rescue
22 Tom Tackles the Chalet School
23 The Chalet School and Rosalie
24 Three Go to the Chalet School
25 The Chalet School and the Island
26 Peggy of the Chalet School
27 Carola Storms the Chalet School
28 The Wrong Chalet School
29 Shocks for the Chalet School
30 The Chalet School in the Oberland

31 Bride Leads the Chalet School
32 Changes for the Chalet School
33 Joey Goes to the Oberland
34 The Chalet School and Barbara
35 The Chalet School Does it Again
36 A Chalet Girl from Kenya
37 Mary-Lou of the Chalet School
38 A Genius at the Chalet School
39 Chalet School Fête
40 A Problem for the Chalet School
41 The New Mistress at the Chalet School
42 Excitements for the Chalet School
43 The Coming of Age of the Chalet School
44 The Chalet School and Richenda
45 Trials for the Chalet School
46 Theodora and the Chalet School
47 Joey & Co in Tirol
48 Ruey Richardson at the Chalet School
49 A Leader in the Chalet School
50 The Chalet School Wins the Trick
51 A Future Chalet School Girl
52 The Feud in the Chalet School
53 The Chalet School Triplets
54 The Chalet School Reunion
55 Jane of the Chalet School
56 Redheads of the Chalet School
57 Adrienne and the Chalet School
58 Summer Term at the Chalet School
59 Challenge for the Chalet School
60 Two Sams at the Chalet School
61 Althea Joins the Chalet School
62 Prefects of the Chalet School

A United Chalet School

Elinor M. Brent-Dyer

This book contains Part II of *The New Chalet School*. Part I is also available in Armada

Armada
An Imprint of HarperCollinsPublishers

Dedicated to Lucy Violet Moore of India
with love from Elinor

First published in a single volume under the title
The New Chalet School in the UK by
W & R Chambers Ltd, Edinburgh
First published in this edition as the second part of
the Armada paperback *The New Chalet School*
in Armada in 1988

This impression 1992

Armada is an imprint of HarperCollins Children's Books,
a division of HarperCollins Publishers Ltd,
77–85 Fulham Palace Road, Hammersmith,
London W6 8JB

Printed and bound in Great Britain by
HarperCollins Book Manufacturing Ltd, Glasgow.

Contents

1   The Middles Make a Stir   7
2   Joey Takes a Hand   15
3   Caught!   26
4   Before the Prefects   35
5   Salzburg   44
6   A Hair-Raising Adventure   57
7   A Queer Night   69
8   One at Last   83

CHAPTER 1

The Middles Make a Stir

"I wonder," mused Hilary Burn, sitting among her fellow Seniors, "what our next excitement will be."

"We don't want any more this term, thank you," said Louise, to whom her remark had been addressed. "The last few weeks have given me excitement enough. I never heard of such a school. If it isn't one thing, it's another. I'll be just as grateful if things go quietly till the end of term."

"Well, that's not six weeks off," said Hilary thoughtfully. "And we're to have the Salzburg trip some weekend soon, so I should think the Middles will have enough to keep them occupied. I know," she added, laughing, "that it *is* the Middles who worry you. The Juniors seem to be quite a meek and mild set."

"I don't know how it is," sighed Louise, "but the best Junior on earth seems to become possessed of a spirit of mischief as soon as she becomes a Middle."

"Oh, it's a mischievous age, that's all," said Anne, joining in the conversation.

"Well, Evvy and Co have reformed," observed Margia, who was sitting beside them, frowning over a piece of thorough-bass. "That's something."

"It might be if there weren't people just as bad to take their place," sighed Louise, who was in a thoroughly pessimistic mood that morning. "Alixe von Elsen is the limit. And everyone says that Elizabeth Arnett and Betty Wynne-Davies are just as bad. I like most of your Junior people, Hilary, but those two really are the edge!"

"They always were. And the worst of it is one never knows where to have them. They do things no one would ever dream of making rules about."

"Elizabeth's going the right way to get herself expelled," said Ida abruptly, from her nook by a tall tree.

"Expelled? What do you mean?" demanded Anne.

"They're breaking dormitory at night."

"How do you know?"

"I've heard them, of course. You know I have a corner cubey with a window. Well, I can't sleep this hot weather, and I've heard people up on St Clare's roof more than once lately. I recognized Elizabeth's dulcet tones among them last night. Unfortunately, I'm not in St Clare's, and by the time I got along there, they'd probably have slung – I mean escaped." Ida stopped, very red, for she had been in trouble that day for her use of slang.

"But how could they?" cried Anne. "The roof garden door is locked every night, and Matron has the keys."

"Couldn't tell you. But they *do*."

"Impossible!" said Louise. 'For one thing, they're all in downstairs dormies, and it would mean going through another dormy, even if they could get out by the windows – which they can't. All those windows were fixed after Alixe and Co *did* go out one night last summer and were caught by Jo Bettany. D'you remember, you people? Jo told us a priceless story about it."

"I remember!" Margia broke into laughter. "Jo caught them and had them in the Moorland dormy, and ticked them off thoroughly. Then she tossed some weird rag-doll they'd been dangling to scare her into a corner, and one of the maids saw it when she went up to open the shutters next morning, and thought it was the devil. That was how Bill got hold of it. She was furious, and Mademoiselle had the windows fixed so that no one could get out by them."

"Well, I can't help it," said Ida stubbornly. "I *heard* them, and what they are doing, goodness knows! Nothing they ought to be, of course."

"Bother them!" Anne looked serious. "If they're

caught, it means an outsize row. Lulu, what d' you think we ought to do?''

"Catch them at it and administer justice ourselves," said Louise. "If the Abbess catches them, there *will* be trouble."

"There will," said Margia with conviction. "She's not what you'd call sweet-tempered these days. What's wrong with her?"

"They're worried about Mademoiselle, I think," said Louise. "I was up at the Sonnalpe this weekend, and I went to see her. She isn't getting on. I'm sure she won't be down next term, anyhow."

The young faces grew serious.

"Is she very bad?" asked Paula.

"She's none too fit, and that's the truth," said Louise. "Say, girls, do you think maybe she isn't coming back at all?"

"Oh, nonsense!" said Anne sharply. 'Of course she is! It's only the hot weather pulling her down. You *are* a pessimist, Lulu!"

But the girls looked graver. It had never dawned on them till now that there might be a chance of Mademoiselle's not returning, and until Louise had voiced her fears, no one had even hinted at it.

"She was very, very ill last autumn," said Paula slowly.

"Here's Gillian coming," said Anne, still with that sharp note in her voice. "She was up last weekend, too. Let's hear what she says."

Gillian came slowly across the grass to them, and dropped down with a sigh of relief into the deck chair Margia pushed towards her. "Oh, what a rest to sit down! I've been having an argument with Alixe, Elizabeth and Betty, and it's too hot for arguments."

"Never mind that," said Anne quickly. "Lulu says that perhaps Mademoiselle may not come back to school again. You were up last weekend. Did you see her? Have you heard anything?"

A troubled look came into Gillian's face. For years she had been a guardian to her sister, Joyce, and her mother's confidante, and she was older than her years. She had been quietly putting two and two together, and she guessed that Mademoiselle's condition was graver than anyone had given the school to understand. Besides, she had heard talks between her mother and sundry of the doctors' wives, and she could not help seeing that at the Sanatorium those in charge thought Mademoiselle very ill. On the other hand, nothing had been said to the girls, and she was not sure how far she could go without betraying confidence. She sat still, one long pigtail dangling over her shoulder into her lap, and said nothing.

"You *do* think so," said Louise shrewdly. "You'd tell us, otherwise."

Gillian tossed back her pigtail and faced them. "It's difficult to know what to say. You see, Frau Mensch and Frau di Bersetti, and Madame Grignon and the others all come to see Mummy, and they talk, and I hear things when I'm serving the coffee. The Head has said nothing to us – no one has – and I don't know if they want us to know. I've thought, of course. But I didn't like to speak."

"You may as well tell us now," said Margia. "Lulu's upset the applecart, and she has only her own ideas to go on. What do *you* think, Gill?"

Gillian was silent. "I think Lulu's right," she said at length. "Mademoiselle isn't making much progress – if any. I've heard them say that the doctors wanted to perform a second operation, but daren't because of her heart. Well, if that's the case, I'm afraid she isn't likely to get better very quickly."

"What do you think will be the end of it?" said Anne insistently.

Gillian gave it up. They would insist on knowing. They might as well know without further fuss.

"I think she will never get really well," she said slowly.

"I heard on Sunday that the Lecoutiers – Simone's folk, you know – are leaving Paris and taking a chalet on the Sonnalpe. Simone is coming here to teach eventually, and while she is at the Sorbonne she is to live with an aunt. It's a big chalet the Lecoutiers are taking, and I believe they are going to let rooms to help out. You know they are very poor. Simone once told me that Mademoiselle was educating her and Renée."

"But do you think – do you mean—?" Louise stopped short. She was unable to say the thing outright.

Gillian took her up quickly. "I believe they think she may live for years. But it will be as an invalid. I'm sure of that."

There was a silence. It was a bad shock, for, except for Louise this last week or so, they had not expected anything like it.

Margia broke the silence. "How – how *ghastly*!" she said in broken tones.

A shadow fell across them, and Miss Wilson was there. "What are you talking about?" she demanded briefly. "What is so ghastly? And why do you all look ready to burst into tears?"

"It's Mademoiselle," said Louise, controlling herself with difficulty.

"Mademoiselle? What do you mean?"

"Oh, Miss Wilson! Mademoiselle is going to get better, isn't she?" pleaded Margia.

Miss Wilson grasped in a moment what they meant. "I cannot tell you that she will be better soon, Margia. She is still very ill, though they hope to pull her through after a time. But she will not be fit to teach for a very long time," she said, choosing her words with care. Then she reminded them that she wanted to see some of them in half an hour or so, and departed, thinking it safer.

Her place was taken by a small girl who came meekly across the grass to them. Louise looked up.

"Well? What do you want?" she asked shortly. "You

children aren't supposed to come here, you know. This is the Senior garden."

Alixe von Elsen lifted grey eyes full of innocence to the speaker's face and replied, 'No, Louise. But Miss Annersley told me to say that she wishes all the Sixth Form to go to Matron's room at once."

The Seniors exchanged glances. "What on earth does this mean?" asked Hilary, when Alixe was safely out of ear-shot.

"You know as much as I do," replied Louise briefly.

"D'you think it's a kind of belated All Fools' joke?" asked Gillian doubtfully. "You never know when Alixe's sense of humour is going to break out, you know."

"I should think it's true," said Anne. "Even Alixe wouldn't dare to send us on a wild goose chase to Matey's room. She knows she'd get into trouble with both sides. We'd better go."

They went, adding several of the two forms on their way, and finally arrived in Matron's room to find that lady awaiting them, Dr Jem beside her, and a case open on the table before him. In the far corner stood Dr Mensch with swabs and sundry bottles on a small table beside him. Miss Annersley was also there, looking very grave. The girls stopped in the doorway, wondering what it was all about.

"Come in, girls," said Dr Jem genially. "No need to be afraid. But there's smallpox about. Two more cases have been reported, and we're vaccinating the entire valley just for safety."

So that was what it was all about. No wonder the Head has been so short in her manner lately!

One by one the girls were questioned as to when they had last been vaccinated, and if it had "taken". Three people had been done within the last five years. All the rest had to be attended to now. The three lucky ones were sent off to the garden. The others went to Gottfried Mensch, who swabbed off their arms, made an impression with a tiny

12

instrument on the place, and then sent them to his colleague, who gave them the vaccine. That done, they had to stand aside till it dried, when they were sent out.

"And that's that!" said Hilary once more, as she forgathered with Louise, Anne, Gillian, Arda, and a Hungarian girl, Cyrilla Maurús. "What next? What are you going to do, Lulu?"

"Hold a prefects' meeting after lessons this afternoon," said Louise grimly.

"Why?" demanded Cyrilla.

"The Middles, of course!"

Cyrilla threw up her hands in horror. "Again! Never have I seen such children – never!"

"Oh, come, Cyrilla," said Paula with a faint grin. "We were not such angels ourselves when we were Middles."

"Yes, but we never were so bad as the present Middles," protested Cyrilla.

Then the bell rang, and they had to go in to lessons, at which they found the staff still much perturbed, and apt to come down heavily on the least mistake.

At the prefects' meeting that afternoon they all discussed Ida's surprising statement, and it was decided that something must be done about it. As Elsie Carr said, the roof garden was strictly forbidden to all girls without special permission and, if the children were caught, in the staff's present frame of mind, they would get into serious trouble.

"But what on earth can they *do* up there?" she wound up plaintively.

"I've no idea," said Ida, to whom this was addressed.

"Let's hope they don't manufacture Baby Voodoos," laughed Gillian. "Once of that was more than enough."

"Whatever it is, it's bound to be something they shouldn't be doing," declared Louise. "Oh, dear! This is my last term here, and I did so hope it would be peaceful, and we've had nothing but fusses ever since it began. I reckon I'll be worn to a frazzle before it's over."

"It's no worse, really, than most prees have had to face," said Anne. "Well, we meet in Louise's room at ten o'clock tonight, then – at least, are we *all* going? For if we are, someone is sure to get wind of it."

"Oh, not all of us," said Elsie. "Besides, we may have to watch for two or three nights. I vote we divide our forces. Ida and Gill can join Louise and Paula for tonight. And if necessary, two other people can take hold with Anne and Arda tomorrow."

"How are we going to settle with the staff?" asked Nancy lazily.

"We'd better tell them the Middles are up to something and we want to see to it ourselves," said Louise. "They like us to do that if we can."

"Then all I can say is, I think the staff here is wonderful. Miss Browne scarcely trusted *her* prees at St Scholastika's to take prep," said Nancy.

"Oh, but we have a lot to do with the government of the school," explained Anne. "Suppose you four trot off and see the Abbess about it?"

"Yes, it had better be her," agreed Hilary. "She's more or less reasonable. If you go to Bill or Charlie in their present frame of mind, they'll squash you badly." It was recognized that this was true, so the deputation departed, and the rest dispersed to their various ploys.

"And may it do the Middles good," said Hilary piously as she sat down to *Les Pensées de Pascal* to do a little work. "They *need* it!"

CHAPTER 2

Joey Takes a Hand

The deputation duly waited on Miss Annersley with their request. She raised her brows when she heard it; but beyond asking them if they felt sure they could deal with the matter themselves, she made no further inquiry. She gave them permission to forgather at St Clare's at ten o'clock, and said that she would see the three mistresses in charge of the house.

"How will Ida and Gillian get back to Ste Thérèse's without waking anyone?" she asked.

"We thought that, if you'd give us permission, Evadne and Ida might change cubicles for once," explained Louise. "Then Ida would be next to the door. Gillian has got a door cubicle. And Paula and I are there on the spot."

"Very well," said the Head. Then she added, "Am I to hear afterwards what has occurred?"

The prefects looked at each other. Then Gillian replied, "Yes; if we may tell you unofficially, please."

Miss Annersley's face relaxed, and she laughed. "I suppose it's something of the same nature as Evadne's jazz band of last summer," she said. "Well, I consider such things are best dealt with by you girls yourselves, so we'll leave it at that. But why couldn't Anne and Arda be on guard instead of having two people from Ste Thérèse's? Surely that would have been more convenient?"

"Oh, it would," agreed Louise. "But Ida found the thing out and warned us. And Gill—"

"And Gill and Ida are friends, and can be very squashing when they like," said Paula. "Besides, some of the sinners are old Saints, and we felt that one of their own prefects had better be there."

"I see," said Miss Annersley. Then she added gently,

"But don't you think, Louise, that it's time you people remembered that you are all one school now? More than half the term is over. Ida is one of *our* prefects." And she smiled at the tall girl.

Ida and Louise went pink at this reminder, and then Ida said impulsively and somewhat incoherently, "Oh, Miss Annersley, I do feel that I'm a real Chaletian! I think all that trouble with the Balbini twins at the beginning of term helped to pull us together and make us really one. But it does make a difference sometimes, on occasions like this."

"I see," said the Head. "Well, girls, you may do as you ask. I will see Miss Wilson and explain to her. I don't suppose either she or any other mistress will object to having one responsibility shifted. This has been a heavy term for all of us – heavier than you know."

There was a pause. Then, just as she was about to dismiss them, Louise said, "Miss Annersley, perhaps we know more than you think. Some of us go rather frequently to the Sonnalpe, you know."

Miss Annersley leaned back in her chair and looked at them. How much did they know or guess? How much should she tell them now? Then she remembered something Matey, beloved tyrant of the whole school, had said that horrible day in November when they had first taken Mademoiselle up to the Sonnalpe – "We don't want our girls to grow up spineless jelly-fish, but strong, helpful women."

"Sit down again, girls," she said. "I think you had best hear the truth."

They sat down and faced her, one or two eagerly; the rest soberly.

"Mademoiselle will never teach again," she said abruptly. "If she were strong enough, they would operate again, and she would be all right. But she is not. The doctors can do much for her by other treatment, but they cannot put her completely right. She has had to face up to the fact

16

that for the rest of her life she must be a semi-invalid. She has taken it as bravely as we should all expect. You girls must do the same. I know how dearly you all – yes, *all* – love her. Be plucky about this for her sake.''

A short silence followed. Then Louise spoke. ''Miss Annersley, are we to keep this to ourselves, or may we tell the rest of the Seniors?''

Miss Annersley nodded. ''Tell the rest of the Seniors, but keep it from the younger girls for the present, please.''

''One thing more, Miss Annersley,'' put in Gillian. ''Don't think me impertinent, please, but are you our Head now?''

Miss Annersley blushed as she replied, ''Yes, Gillian.''

''That's good,'' said Hilary, speaking for the first time. ''Of course, we all love Mademoiselle, as you say. But if we can't have her, we're jolly glad to have you.''

Miss Annersley was badly embarrassed by this. She made haste to send the girls off to break the news to the others, and then turned to her letters once more.

Meanwhile, at Louise's suggestion, all the Seniors were summoned to the common room at Ste Thérère's, and there, mounted on a table, she told them what the new Head had said. It was a shock to all, for they had hoped that sooner or later Mademoiselle would be able to resume her duties. But the worst shock was felt by Cornelia Flower. An American girl, motherless from her early babyhood, and spoilt by her father, she had had most of her ''mothering'' from Mademoiselle, and, beneath a flippant exterior, cherished a deep affection for the kindly, plain-faced Frenchwoman whose influence had done so much to turn her from a regular fire-brand into a responsible member of society. Corney, as they called her, rarely talked of deeper things. Only once had she ever unburdened herself – to Jo Bettany. Jo was not here now, and there was no one else. Corney waited till Louise had finished, and then slipped off to the woods, and had it out by herself, hidden from view among the roots of a giant tree. Her friends missed her, but had no idea where she was, so had to leave it. She came back for Abendessen, rather white, and very silent, refusing to discuss the news with anyone. "Guess I've got a headache," she said. "I'll go ask Matey for something, and go to bed."

"I'll come with you," suggested Evadne Lannis, her chum; but Cornelia shook her yellow head.

"I'll be best alone, I guess. You stay here, Evvy."

Matron, who knew all about it – was there *anything* in the school Matey did not know? – agreed to her going to bed, but refused any medicine. 'Sleep is your best medicine, Corney," she said, in softer tones than most people heard from her. "I'll bring you some hot milk when you're in bed."

Cornelia departed, and Matron arrived half an hour later with the milk; saw her take it; then made her lie down, covered her up, and, stooping, kissed her. "I know, Corney," she said. "I've only this for you, child. As one door shuts, another opens. And Mademoiselle wants you girls to face it as bravely as she is doing. Goodnight, dear."

Cornelia turned enormous blue eyes on her. "Guess I – feel 'sif – my mother—" She stopped, unable to go further; and Matron, with a final pat, left her, knowing that Corney would feel everlastingly disgraced if anyone saw her cry.

All the same, the coming years were to show her a true prophetess, and Cornelia was to have such mothering as even Mademoiselle had never given her.

Meanwhile, the prefects to be on duty in St Clare's after Lights Out were clustered together in Miss Wilson's study, that lady having shown herself unexpectedly accommodating, suggesting to Miss Annersley that she should have a camp bed in Miss Stewart's room, and another should be put down in hers, so that Ida and Gillian need not go back to Ste Thérèse's at all that night.

"Better not risk waking the others," she said.

"Or couldn't the camp beds come into Paula's room and mine, Miss Wilson?" proposed Louise. "It seems really mean to have to turn you out."

Miss Wilson shook her head. "My room and Miss Stewart's are much larger than yours, Louise. No, we'll stick to my plan."

So it was arranged; and when ten o'clock came, Gillian and Ida slipped along the connecting passage, carrying what they needed for the night, to find that Bill had provided hot chocolate and buns in her pretty study, while she herself was just off to bed, being tired after a strenuous day. "Don't be too late," she said, "and don't forget to switch off the lights. Gute Nacht!" And she ran off laughing.

"I reckon it won't be much beyond midnight," said Louise, settling into a comfortable chair. "Say! Bill's not hygienic! Look at those thick curtains over the window!"

"Look at your thick head! That's to keep the Middles from seeing our light," said Gillian.

"But how could they see these windows from the roof garden?" protested Ida.

"They could see the glow on the ground outside, couldn't they?" asked Gillian scornfully.

"I hadn't thought of that," admitted Ida.

"Never mind that! Have a bun, Gillian," suggested Louise.

Gillian took a bun and handed the dish to Paula who was curled up on a low padded seat. Paula took it, and looked over its contents. She was about to take the bun of her choice, when there came a sudden tap at the window which made her drop the lot, while the others sprang to their feet, startled for the moment.

"Bill! Are you there?" asked a low-pitched voice, which, nevertheless, they recognized.

"Jo!" gasped Louise. She ran to the window, and drew

back one curtain. "Joey! What on earth are you doing here at this time of night? Come right in, and don't make a sound!"

"What on earth are *you* doing, if it comes to that?" demanded Jo with a startled look as she came in, and Louise let the curtain fall. "What *is* the meaning of this – this gorge in Bill's own study? And where *is* Bill? Am I in topsy-turvy land?"

"No; it's all right, whatever it looks," said Gillian, pulling up a chair. "The Middles are on the rampage and we're out to catch them. We don't want the staff in it, though naturally we've had to tell them something. They agreed to let us tackle it ourselves. As Bill says, certain crimes they *must* punish in certain ways, and if we, as prefects, can save them that, so much the better."

"What have they been doing?" asked Jo curiously as she took the cup of chocolate Louise had poured out for her, and watched Ida and Paula collecting the buns on the floor. "You'll have to sweep that mess up before you leave," she added in parenthesis. "Thanks, Ida, I'll have that iced sponge affair."

Ida handed her the bun, and set the plate on the table. "I'll have to get another cup," she said. "Don't drink all the choco while I'm gone."

"No need to rootle the prees' room at this hour," said Jo. "I know where Bill keeps her crockery. There you are! Take it, and I'll explain to her tomorrow."

"But what are you doing here?" demanded Louise as she filled the cup.

"I'm too late to get back home, so I thought I'd drop in here and see if I could scrounge a bed," explained Jo. "Where's Bill? She's generally rather a late bird."

"Went off early, saying she was tired. She's sleeping with Charlie anyhow," explained Gillian. "Ida and I are to have her bedroom – when the fun's over."

Jo drank her chocolate and handed the cup to Louise for

fresh supplies. "What's going to happen next? And why are Gill and Ida in it? Wouldn't Anne and Arda do? Or are they away, by any chance? In which case, why not use *their* rooms?"

"Jo, you'll turn into a question-mark if you aren't careful!" said Gillian.

"Tell me the story, then, and hurry up!" commanded Jo.

"I reckon we'd better. And do keep your voices down, or those imps will hear us, and then goodbye to any chance of catching them!" said Louise. "The Abbess and Bill have been really sweet about it tonight; but I reckon it won't go on if we have to ask many more favours."

Thus warned, they contrived to speak softly and tell the story one at a time. Jo listened, whistling when it was ended. Then she said calmly, "Well, I'm in on this – of course I am!" as they protested. "What do *you* think? Tell me where I can find a bed, Lulu, and you'll have to lend me pyjamas and a comb among you. Matey will sell me a tooth-brush and paste tomorrow, so I'll be all right."

"I don't know where you can go," said Louise.

"She can share Bill's bed with me," said Gillian. "Ida can have the camp bed. Luckily we two are scrags, and Bill's bed is three-quarter size, so we can manage."

"Good idea," said Jo. Then she chuckled. "Won't Bill get a shock when she sees me at Frühstück? She'll think she's gone back a year!"

"But what have you been doing?" persisted Paula.

"Spent the evening at the Adalbert with the Dennys. I left about half-past eight, and encountered a lost child. She was French, poor mite, and couldn't speak a word of German, so I had to find out which hotel she belonged to. By the time I'd got her consoled, and found out she was at the Stephanie and taken her there, it was nearly ten, so I rang my sister up and said I'd spend the night here."

"And came and found us instead of Bill," supplemented Paula.

"As you say. What's that?"

They held their breath and listened, but it was only the whirring of the grandfather clock outside, giving notice to strike, so they went on with their conversation.

"Shades of last year! I didn't know I was going to drop into anything so thrilling as a Middles' rag," said Jo. "This *is* like old times – only *we* never used Bill's study; *nor* were fed by her on buns and chocolate," she added in injured tones.

"No; *you* used to do things off your own bat," retorted Gillian. "*We* asked permission."

"Yes; and I don't know where you got your nerve. Imagine asking if you could have Bill's own study—"

"We never did! She offered it to us herself!"

"If you folk yell like that, we'll catch no one tonight," said Louise warningly.

"Shan't we? Just listen!" Jo's quick ear had caught a slight sound and now the others heard it. "Someone moving about overhead – the Wheatfield, isn't it? Who's there now?"

"Oh, Elizabeth Arnett, Betty Wynne-Davies, Emmie Linders, Alixe von Elsen, Biddy O'Ryan, and the rest."

"I don't know about Elizabeth and Betty; they're new since my time. But any room that has Alixe, Emmie, and Biddy in it must be fairly enterprising. I haven't forgotten how Biddy told them spooky tales, and Alixe walked in her sleep afterwards and scared me out of nearly a year's growth."

"Do you remember when Alixe made noises outside prep room and you caught her?" asked Paula.

"Rather! How sheepish she looked! Listen! There goes a door! Do the little asses want to bring Bill and Co into it?"

"It sounds loud because we're listening for it," said Gillian shrewdly. "I don't suppose anyone asleep would notice. Shall we go?"

"No; wait till they're all there, and then we'll go up and net the lot," said Louise authoritatively.

"Then take my tip and make sure they can't escape by

any windows," said Jo. "Oh, but Mademoiselle had them all barred, didn't she? Then how have they got out?"

"They were done after that Baby Voodoo business you were mixed up in," said Louise.

Jo chuckled. "I wish you'd seen those kids' faces when they saw me through the door! They'd been getting more and more scared, what with shadows, and a hunting owl, and their own priceless creation. *I* was the last straw! Even Alixe had the starch taken out of her for once."

"I can believe it," murmured Paula. "You were never nice to meet, Jo, when one had an evil conscience."

"I never meant to be," said Jo; adding most immodestly, "and I always succeeded."

"I'll say you did." Louise sounded emphatic. "Say, girls, how much longer d'you think we ought to give them? Ten minutes?"

Jo glanced at her watch. "Just a quarter to eleven. Let's give them till the hour, and then we'll have to risk loiterers; though I don't suppose there are any. They'll get the shock of their young lives, won't they?" said she with a chuckle. "What are you going to do about it, anyhow?"

"Haven't decided yet. We must wait and see what they're doing," said Ida. "It's fairly sure to be something they oughtn't. When Elizabeth and Betty are in anything you can be certain of that!"

"Goodness me! What characters you give your Middles!"

"It's a mystery to me how any decent school was ever persuaded to take them. All they live for is wickedness. Elizabeth *thinks* of the things, and Betty *does* them – with frills on."

"And that sort of thing is added to what we had already in the way of Alixe and Co?" exclaimed Jo with horror. "Well! This school *must* be a pleasing place for the good and mild!"

"We'll settle them," said Louise. "It may be some quite harmless thing, of course."

"Not with Elizabeth and Betty!" put in Ida.

"Perhaps they're midnighting," suggested Jo.

Gillian shook her head. "Never after Joyce's experience! It's still held up as an Awful Example of what happens when you feed out of proper hours."

"And they can't be trying the Baby Voodoo business again. What *can* it be?" wondered Jo.

"Well, it's just on time, so suppose we start off," suggested Louise. "Leave your songs here, Joey. You don't want to carry them up to the top of the house."

Jo dropped her music case behind a chair. "That's safe enough. Are we going to shut the windows before we go?"

"Yes, we'd better, I think. Switch off the light, someone, and I'll latch them." Louise waited till they were in darkness. Then she shut the windows, and they all left the study very quietly.

"No more talking," commanded the Head Girl. "We don't want to disturb anyone."

They stole up the stairs in silence, and along the wide corridor which led to the upper flight. Arrived there, they went up on tiptoe, ready in case the Middles should have thought of posting a sentry. But those young persons had never dreamed of taking such precautions, and the little band reached the top storey without incident.

"Pinewoods, first," said Louise, switching on her torch. "You wait here, and I'll see if they're there or not." She carefully turned the handle of the nearest door, and slipped into the room. A minute later she returned, shaking her head. "They've nothing to do with it – all sound asleep. I'm glad of that. They're all junior Middles in there. Now try Moorlands."

Moorlands dormitory proved to be empty. Louise, stooping nearly double, crawled to the window, and looked out on a festive scene. She hurried back, drawing the door to after her, and locking it.

"Well?" demanded Ida.

"A crowd of them out there. But they didn't get through the window. We'd better try the store room. I don't believe that window was done – though how they got in when it's always kept locked beats me!"

The store room was not locked, however, and Louise, taking the key from the keyhole, gave an exclamation. "It opens with the same key as Moorlands! Oh, the little wretches! I shall report this to Matron in the morning. She'll get the lock changed tomorrow, or I'm much mistaken. And the window is wide open, so that's how they got out. Hold my torch, Jo. I'm going to fasten that window."

Jo took the torch, and Louise crept across the room and closed the window cautiously. She need not have feared detection. The girls were too much interested in what was going on in front of them to bother about what happened behind. Most of them sat in a solid phalanx, facing to the north, where a blaze of light poured upon a group of three gesticulating figures.

The Head Girl joined her compeers, and told them what she had seen. "And what they can be doing is more than I can say," she wound up.

Gillian was quicker. "It must be an entertainment of some sort."

Jo gripped her arm. "Got it! The *imps*! Don't you see? It's some sort of dramatic club we've stumbled on; and quite a good idea, too, if they held it at a proper hour."

"Not so far as Betty and Elizabeth are concerned," muttered Ida.

"Come on!" said Louise, making for the part-glassed-in door which led to the roof garden. "I'm going out to them."

She straightened herself to her fullest height, unlocked and flung open the door, and stalked forth into the midst of a crowd of such flabbergasted Middles as even Jo the experienced had never before seen.

CHAPTER 3

Caught!

As Jo had grasped at once, they had arrived at the beginning of a play. The majority of the girls were sitting with their backs to the door, for they were in slantwise formation. They were fully dressed, which meant that they had slipped pyjama jackets over their underclothes, and when they got up simply put on frocks and blazers again.

A row of flashlights were arranged before this audience, and in the glare of the lights stood three people attired in what was meant to be period costume. One wore her frock caught up in front to make panniers. Another was wrapped in a huge shawl which covered her from head to foot, leaned on a stick, and wore a hood which later turned out to be a linen bag. The last wore a jacket turned inside out to show the lining, and gym knickers. Her thick red locks were tied back in a pigtail, and she was plainly the hero of the piece.

"Alixe – and Elizabeth. Who on earth is the old woman?" whispered Gillian to Ida.

"Betty, for a ducat! Who are the people at the back?"

Gillian peered through the surrounding gloom, for the torches illuminated little more than the "stage". "Biddy O'Ryan and Emmie Linders, from the general appearance. I think that other one is either Nicole de Saumarez or Elsa Fischer."

Meanwhile, Louise had gone forward, demanding, "What are you doing here at this hour – or at all?"

There was silence for a moment. Then the "old woman" straightened up and advanced, throwing off her hood, and showing the impudent face of Betty Wynne-Davies.

"Hello, Louise!" she said pertly. "Have *you* come to

26

join the happy throng? I didn't think *prefects* would break rules, whatever we might do."

"Be quiet!" said Louise sternly. "You aren't doing yourself any good by this, Betty."

"I told you so," murmured Ida to Gillian. "Come along, we can't leave it all to Louise." And she marched forward, followed by Gillian, Paula, and Jo.

Louise had turned to Alixe von Elsen. "What are you doing, Alixe?"

Alixe glanced at her fellow actors and seemed to gather courage from their return looks. "Acting, Louise," she said blandly.

"And what if Miss Wilson comes?" asked Paula with equal blandness.

Alixe turned round with a start. She had not seen anyone but Louise, and the sight of three other prefects and Jo took some of her assurance from her.

"Miss Wilson knows nothing about it," retorted Betty for her. "Unless you sneak, that is," she added.

"Don't talk rot!" Ida took a hand. "You know quite well the difference between sneaking and reporting, so don't pretend you don't!"

"Well? What are you going to do about it?" demanded Elizabeth.

"Find out what you are doing; send you to bed; deal with it tomorrow," Louise told her succinctly. "Hurry up! I don't intend to stay here all night!"

"And if we *don't* tell you? queried Betty.

'Then it'll go to Miss Annersley and Miss Wilson," said Jo, joining in. "I don't know about you and Elizabeth, Betty, but I can imagine what Alixe and Emmie and some of the others will have to face if it comes to that. *You* people may get off with a lecture and order marks, as you're more or less new. But perhaps you counted on that?" She finished on a note of polite interrogation which was maddening.

Neither Elizabeth nor Betty had met Jo in this light before, and they rose to her remark at once.

"No, we didn't!" retorted Betty. "If there's a row, we're all in it – share and share alike! So there!"

"That will rather depend on the staff, though." Jo spoke with polite interest.

"If we explain—' began Elizabeth, who lacked some of her boon companion's native impudence.

"Tell them," said Louise, "and I reckon you'll get more than you bargain for."

"Then they'll be jolly unfair!" flashed Betty.

"Not at all. Any girl who has been more than a term at the Chalet knows exactly how far she may go. She also knows the penalties for breaking certain rules. If she likes to take her fun and pay for it, that's her concern. Alixe and the rest all know exactly what they've been doing in the way of rule-breaking. They also know the punishment. I presume they're prepared to pay. You people can't be expected to know. You're new this term, and, apparently, you're remarkably stupid," said Gillian.

"Stupid?" came a protest from the audience.

"Yes, *very* stupid, or you'd have guessed what this sort of thing would lead to."

"That's enough," said Louise, as fresh murmurs rose. "If you make that noise, you'll soon have Miss Wilson or Miss Stewart or Miss Nalder on your track – to say nothing of Matron."

The girls were silent. No one seemed to have any answer, and one or two looked ready to burst into tears. Louise, having given her own and Gillian's remark time to sink in, was about to order them off the roof, when through the open doorway irrupted a bright-haired vision in a lurid dressing-gown. "Say!" it exclaimed in clarion tones, "I guess you kids had best vamoose, p. d. q., or you'll know all about it! And you can report to Louise tomorrow for breaking dormy af— Great snakes! *Joey!*"

28

"If you *want* to bring the staff on this pleasant scene, Corney, I'd go on yelling like that," said Jo calmly. "Louise is here already, and so are Gill, Paula, and Ida – plenty of prefects, you see. I only dropped in accidentally."

"Well, say, I'm real glad you're here," announced Corney, dropping her voice. "I guess these little—'

"You be careful," Jo warned her. "It might be as well not to air the brighter parts of your vocabulary at this moment."

Brought up short a second time, Cornelia fell silent, and Louise proceeded to order the delinquents back to bed.

"And go quietly if you don't want the staff to hear you and come up," she warned them. "Elsa, lead the way!"

Elsa Fischer, looking ready to cry, left the company and departed to her cubicle in Moorlands, where she speedily buried herself beneath the sheets and wept copiously. The rest followed in twos and threes, Louise not being minded to risk a stampede and the consequent arrival of any of the staff. Paula stood at the doorway, scribbling down the names in her notebook, and Gillian and Ida were at different points on the stairs to prevent any further trouble. Finally, the only ones left were Biddy O'Ryan, Elizabeth Arnett, Betty Wynne-Davies, Emmie Linders, and Alixe von Elsen.

"How did you Wheatfield people get here?" asked Louise.

"By the fire escape, and through that empty maids' room opposite the storeroom," said Emmie in a shaking voice. Three terms or so ago she had got herself into various scrapes, and the subsequent report that had gone home had involved her in an outsize row. She could quite imagine what would happen if her father got wind of tonight's escapade, and she shook in her shoes at the bare thought.

"So that's how you managed," said Jo. "I wondered how such a pack of you had got here without being caught.

Louise, don't you think it might be as well to send them back the same way?"

Emmie broke down at this. After all, she was only thirteen, and she had had broken sleep for the past three nights, for, as the elder girls later discovered, this had been going on all the week.

Louise gave her a gentle shake. "Stop that!" she said. "Crying won't help matters."

Emmie gulped down her tears, and stood silent, except for an occasional sniff. Louise turned to the rest. "Whose bright idea was it?"

"Mine," said Elizabeth defiantly.

"It didn't need much guessing for *that*," said Ida. "I knew you were at the bottom of it."

Elizabeth was silent, but Betty was still uncowed. "If you knew, why ask?" she demanded with the cool impudence which had reduced the St Scholastika prefects to such impotent wrath during the past year.

But the St Scholastika prefects and the Chalet School prefects were two different bodies. Miss Browne had always insisted on being consulted by her prefects before any decision was made. The Heads of the Chalet School expected theirs to be able to cope with most things without reference to them, though they were always ready to help and advise. Consequently, instead of flaring up, Louise merely eyed the small girl with an expression which contrived to show that *any* prefect was miles above any Middle, and the Head Girl rather more so. Despite herself, Betty went red, and began to wish she had not been quite so impudent.

"I'll see you tomorrow," said Louise, after an interval calculated to strike terror into the heart of the cheekiest Middle. "I've only one more question for tonight. Did you do anything besides give plays?"

"No-o-o," said Elizabeth hesitatingly.

"D'you mean that?" demanded Jo suspiciously.

"Well, I don't quite know what Louise means."

"Did you bring any food up?" asked Louise.

The five small girls looked at each other despairingly. Oh, wasn't Louise *awful*! They had hoped to escape this question.

"All right, Louise," said Gillian. "They did! Where is it?"

"Over there," said Alixe, nodding to the far corner.

"All right, Louise. I'll see to it while you pack these beauties off to bed," said Jo. "Corney, too, by the way. I'd like to know what you were doing awake at this hour, Corney, but it can wait till the morning. Meantime, Gill and Ida and I will investigate the food question."

Louise glanced at her watch, and discovered to her horror that it was after midnight. She hurriedly marshalled the five into line, and, aided by Paula, walked them off to their dormitory. Cornelia stayed where she was. She wanted a word with Joey. While the elder girls examined the refreshments, she curled herself up in a wicker chair and waited.

"Chocs – sweets – ginger – fruit – and *a packet of cigarettes*!" Jo spoke the last words in italics. "Well, if ever Bill or the Abbess gets wind of this, I'm sorry for the culprits!"

"Have they had any? The packet's been opened," said Gillian.

Jo looked. "One gone. I wonder who was the victim?" Suddenly she crumpled up into laughter. "It's almost a pity we didn't wait till they'd all sampled them. They'd have learnt a lesson then!"

"But you smoke yourself, Joey," said Gillian. "I've seen you."

"Oh, yes – once in a blue moon. And always decent stuff. This is cheap tobacco. I should think if those Middies had tackled them they'd have been ready to die!"

"Someone *has* tackled one of them," Gillian pointed out.

"Then I hope she did feel ready to die," said Jo

31

unsympathetically. "The very idea of babes of that age trying to smoke!"

"They're like small boys, I suppose," said Ida. "See their grown-ups with cigarettes, and want to do the same. I never remember wanting to try myself, though I've seen my mother and aunts dozens of times. But perhaps their generation is different."

"More than likely," said Jo. "Here, Corney! You're younger. Ever want to smoke?"

"I guess *not*!" Corney spoke emphatically. "When I was a kid, I got hold of one of Poppa's cigars and had a go at it. Gee! I never was sicker in my life! And he caught me at it and gave me a good switching later on!"

"I should think that *would* end your researches into the effect of tobacco," agreed Jo. "Yes, I can quite see that cigarettes wouldn't be in your line."

"Well," said Gillian, "we can't do any good here. We'd better collect this stuff and dispose of it somewhere till morning. Then we can settle how we'll deal with those imps."

"You and Ida go on," said Cornelia. "I want to speak to Jo."

"Right!" said Jo. "At the same time, Corney, you've no real right here, and if you're caught there'll be a fuss."

"I know, but I guess I can stand it," said Cornelia philosophically.

"We're going," said Gillian. "Don't be too long, though, Jo. Or if you're a while, try not to wake us, won't you? We'll be dead tomorrow!"

"I shan't be more than a minute or two," said Jo. "Tell me quickly what you want, Corney."

Cornelia stood twisting a corner of her dressing-gown between her fingers until Gillian and Ida had departed. With some idea of being useful and giving the younger girl time to collect herself, Jo stooped down and began to gather up the torches. Some of them had given up the ghost already. She switched off the rest, and tossed the lot into one of the basket chairs. Suddenly she felt two hands closing on one arm, and turned to look down into Cornelia's wide, frightened eyes.

"What's wrong, Corney?" she asked gently.

"It's Mademoiselle!" panted Cornelia. "Oh, Joey, they're not keeping anything from us? She – she won't – *die*?"

Jo put an arm round her. Cornelia clung to her desperately, shaking all over.

"She *will* get better – won't she?" she asked.

Jo's beautiful eyes were very soft as she looked down on the yellow head at her shoulder. "Humanly speaking, Corney, she's likely to live for years. She will never be well and strong again, but the doctors all agree that she may live to be an old woman." Then, as she felt the sobs shaking Cornelia, she added, 'Corney, it's frightfully late, and you ought to be in bed. Come along and I'll see you to your dormy. Oh, you poor old girl! What a ghastly time you've had over this!"

Cornelia had a strong will. Resolutely she drove back the tears, and presently was able to look up at Jo and say, "Thanks, Jo, but I guess I can sleep now. And you'll talk to me in the morning?"

"It's morning now. There's one o'clock chiming. But I'll see you at break tomorrow. I must go home and change, but I'll come back. Now come to bed – do! I've got to share Bill's bed with Gill, and goodness knows how we'll ever fit in!"

A wavering smile came over Cornelia's face at this. "It's a real good thing you're both skinny," she said. "All right, Joey. You needn't bother to come with me. I can manage."

"Sure? All right, then. Oh! and Corney, don't say anything to anyone about tonight, will you? I mean, it really is the prees' affair."

"Take me for a fool?" demanded Cornelia indignantly.

33

"I can be as dumb as a fish if I like. Goodnight, Jo. Thanks awfully for being so decent to me. I feel better now."

"Goodnight, old thing!" Joey carefully extinguished the last torch, which had rolled into a corner, and tossed it onto the pile before she retired to Miss Wilson's room, to find Ida and Gillian just getting into bed, and relieved that she had come so soon. The rest of the night was devoted to Gillian and herself giving a good imitation of two sardines in a box. Still, as both were sleepy, it made no difference to them in the end, and Gillian had to be shaken awake in the morning.

CHAPTER 4

Before the Prefects

"Joey, do think and tell us something that will settle that crew for good and all!" Thus Anne at the beginning of the prefects' meeting which was held after break next morning to decide what they should do about the last night's excitement. Joey, bidden to the assembly by virtue of having been among the captors of the previous night, had cycled round the lake after she had rushed home to change into something more suitable than a light dinner dress, and to tell her sister a hurried tale of what had happened. She had taken longer than she had intended and had arrived late for the meeting, which, by grace of the Head, was to be held during Mademoiselle Berné's lesson, that lady being laid low with a migraine to which she was occasionally subject.

Joey cast herself into the chair reserved for her between Paula and Hilary, and wrinkled her brows. "Something that will settle them for good and all? What a hope! As if Middles ever *were* settled for good and all. The only thing that seems to make any difference, so far as I can see, is becoming Seniors. Then they do seem to learn a little common sense. But I defy you to find anything that will be a permanent check on the ill-doings of the average Middle."

"I don't know," said Anne reminiscently. "As Gill often says, there has been no more midnighting since Joyce and that little wretch Mary Shaw were so ill in February last year."

Gillian laughed. "Joyce got such a lesson then that she's been careful about what and when she eats ever since."

Louise nodded. "I reckon Joyce is one of the steadiest of the younger Seniors we have today."

Jo laughed. "And I can assure you I've never attempted

to powder anyone's hair with cornflour since I had the joy of washing it out myself next day.''

"How angry Lonny and Yvette were!" said Paula. "They both have such long hair, and so much, and it was such a long time before the cornflour was washed out.''

"But all this has nothing to do with last night's affair," said Ida impatiently, for these were past pranks in which she had no interest. "We must do something! Those little wretches can't be allowed to think they can go on like that!''

"I should think not!" exclaimed Paula. "Cigarettes, indeed! And at their age!''

"That's something *we* never thought of," said Elsie Carr.

"We had too much sense," retorted her *alter ego*, Margia Stevens.

Louise rapped on the table. "We can't waste our time in discussion. And anyway, this isn't free conversation, it's a meeting. I reckon we'll get on faster if you all agree to address the Chair only.''

There was a pause. Then Hilary rose. "Did I understand, Madam Chairwoman – is that the way to address the Chair, by the way? – that *one* cigarette had been smoked?''

"The packet was one short, anyhow," said Louise.

"I wonder who did it?" murmured Cyrilla Maurús. "I am sorry for her whoever she is.''

"Why do you want to know, Hilary?" asked Louise.

"I was just thinking – but no, you couldn't do it at school," said Hilary rather maddeningly.

"Couldn't do what?''

"Make the lot share them and smoke – since they *want* to smoke, evidently, or they wouldn't have wasted their money on them.''

Jo rocked with laughter. "How rich it would be! But of course you are right. It would be an original punishment – but a bit *too* original for the staff, I'm afraid. Can't you hear Matey on the subject?''

"It would serve them right if we did it, all the same,"

declared Ida vindictively. "Horrid little things! It's high time we showed them that that sort of thing isn't *done* here!"

Jo said nothing but it flashed across her mind that until the enterprising Balbini twins had declared war on the school, the old "Saints" had never thought in quite such terms. The twins had caused trouble enough, but they had effected that much good!

"We can't possibly set those imps to smoking," said Louise, horror in her voice. "Do think of something really sensible, someone! We don't want to report them if it can be helped. Lots of them are new this term, and there's no point in giving them a bad beginning if we can help it."

"Lines would be no use," said Margia thoughtfully.

"Not in the least," agreed Hilary cheerfully. "It would take a lot more than lines to settle the Elizabeth-Betty combine. Goodness knows, they must have got plenty of those at St Scholastika's, but I never saw that it did them any good."

"Then what else do you propose?" asked Cryilla. "We cannot do nothing, you know."

"I have an idea,' announced Nancy Wilmot sleepily.

"What's that?" asked Louise hopefully.

"Well, why not ask the Head's permission to have the use of Hall tonight? Then we can send for them, *after* Kaffee und Kuchen, mind, and tell them they've got to give that play of theirs tonight, immediately after Abendessen, and to the entire school."

There was a silence.

"But is that not what they would like?" asked Paula hesitatingly.

Nancy shook her head. "Some of them mayn't mind; but most of them will; especially if we say that they are to find parts for all. They can't have rehearsed very much, and it will be before the *whole* school – babies and all! Did *you* enjoy making a fool of yourself before your juniors at that age?"

"I did *not*," said Elsie emphatically.

Pure delight illuminated Jo's face. "It's a stroke of

genius! And apart from anything else, if they don't come up to scratch, their own clan won't forget to let them hear of it."

Cyrilla rose with dignity. "May I add to the suggestion?"

"If you can," said Louise.

"Well, then, I propose we say that they must also provide refreshments for the audience."

"How on earth can they do that?" asked Anne.

"They all have cakes and sweets in their hampers. We will tell them that they must go to Matron for them and use those," said Cyrilla. "It is so near the end of term that many of them will not get any more, and they don't get enough pocket money to supply very much, do they?"

"No – and we are forbidden to enter any shops for the next week or two. The notice was on the board just before break," said Louise slowly.

"Well!" said Joey. "If *that* doesn't teach them, I don't know what will! Got to make themselves look silly! Deprived of tuck! It's a scorching punishment!"

"But will they do it, do you think?" asked Ida. "You people don't know what Elizabeth and Betty can be like."

"It'll be a choice between that and a Head's report," said Louise shortly. 'I should think even such criminals as you make those two out to be would shy at that."

Ida looked sceptical. "I don't suppose a little thing like a Head's report will bother that pair very much."

"It mayn't – till they know what it means," agreed Anne. "But I can tell you that people like Biddy and Alixe will never agree to being reported if there is an alternative. They'll force those two to give in."

"Why? Is a report such a very dreadful thing?" asked Hilary.

Joey began to count off on her fingers. "One: you're gated for a longer or shorter period. Two: you lose all privileges, such as fiction from the library, exeats, and so on. Three: no Kaffee und Kuchen out of doors. Four: no going to camp – and lots more little things like that. Those are more or less invariable. The rest depends on what the crime was. But none of it's nice.''

'Oh! What an awfully *inclusive* business! Yes, Anne, you're right. I don't see anyone choosing that to even such an idea as ours.''

So it was settled. Joey departed, promising to return in the evening to see the play, though she declined an invitation to the prefects' meeting, pointing out that such things were no business of hers now. The prefects took out *Mon Petit Trott*, their set book for translation at present, and got on with as much as they could until the bell rang. Louise alone occupied herself in something else – the writing of the notice which would summon the sinners to the prefects' room after Kaffee und Kuchen to hear their sentence.

Miss Annersley, duly approached after Mittagessen, agreed that Hall might be used. Wisely, she asked no questions, and only promised that she would be there, and would request as many of the staff as could to accompany her.

''Not Mademoiselle Berné, I'm afraid,' she said. ''She is too poorly for anything of the kind. And the Juniors, Louise? My dear girl, do you think it really necessary to have them?''

''I think it might be as well,'' said Louise slowly. ''You see, Miss Annersley, this isn't an ordinary kind of show. It's by way of being a punishment.''

''A punishment?'' Miss Annersley's eyebrows rose. ''I don't understand, Louise. Have these girls been having plays out of hours?''

''Yes,'' acknowledged Louise. Then, fervently, ''Oh, Miss Annersley, if you *wouldn't* mind not asking questions! It would be so kind of you!''

The piercing grey eyes that had never yet needed glasses looked at her, and Louise felt herself go scarlet.

''I don't mean to be rude – it isn't that. But – but—'' she

came to a full stop, not very sure how to continue.

"I see," said the Head. "Very well, Louise. I will ask no more questions. But if you want the Juniors present at this affair, we must have Abendessen half an hour earlier. Preparation will begin immediately after Kaffee and Kuchen."

"Thank you," said Louise gratefully.

"You had better go and inform the other prefects, unless you have anything else to tell me."

"No, that's all, thank you," said Louise, rising. She made the usual curtsey, and departed, thankful that the Head had been so reasonable.

The girls were startled when they read the notice put up that afternoon, but even Betty and Co had no idea that it had any reference to their last escapade. But their faces fell when they saw the one beneath written in Louise's firm black script.

NOTICE

The following girls will report to the prefects' room immediately after Kaffee und Kuchen this afternoon.

LOUISE V. REDFIELD.

Beneath came a long list of names – all those who had been on the roof garden the night before.

"What on earth's going to happen?" demanded Hilda Imray, a former "Saint".

"Louise and the prefects will tell us our punishment. Oh, dear!" said Elsa Fischer dejectedly.

"Funking?" jeered Elizabeth. "They can't slay us! I suppose it means endless lines, but it's been worth it."

"It won't be lines," said Kitty Burnett. "We don't have them here – or only for very small things. And the prees can do a good deal, my child, as you'll find out before long."

"So long as it is not a Head's report," said Emmie Linders. "But if it is that—"

"Don't be silly! If it had been, you'd have been up before

40

now," said Kitty kindly. "And I must say, Emmie, you people deserve all you'll get."

"*All*? What *can* they do? Only jaw us," said Elizabeth, with decided vulgarity.

"That's all you know, as I've told you before," retorted Kitty.

"Then what price a Head's report?"

At once a babbling crowd began to explain to them just what a Head's report meant at the Chalet School. The newcomers listened with faces growing longer and longer.

"Oh, my hat!" gasped Elizabeth at length. "What a ghastly show! Do you really mean to say that there's all that in it? Why, Miss Browne never did anything but jaw us till she was blue in the face and then give us order marks. Fat lot we cared, too!"

"Slang, Elizabeth? Ten groschen to the box!" said a cold voice behind them, and the Middles turned to find Paula von Rothenfels glaring at them.

"Oh, *blow!*" muttered Elizabeth rebelliously. "As if a bit of chat like that *mattered*!" But she was careful not to say it aloud, and Paula took no notice of her mutterings. She left the group, and Elizabeth went sulkily away to pay her fine.

Promptly after Kaffee und Kuchen the Middles filed upstairs to the prefects' room, where they knocked jauntily at the door, and were admitted by Nancy Wilmot. Headed by Elizabeth, they entered the room and faced the grandees of the school, some of them with a certain amount of assurance, the majority with more or less trepidation.

Once they were standing there with the eyes of the thirteen girls who were principally responsible for order in the school fixed on them, even Elizabeth and Betty wilted a little. At St Scholastika's, the prefects had had very little responsibility. In the Chalet School it was different, and the "Saints" dismally reflected that they had had no idea that prees could look so imposing. Indeed, Elizabeth began to wonder if it *would* mean a Head's report, and to think she would almost prefer it to this ordeal.

Louise wasted no time. "We have sent for you to tell you your punishment for last night's affair. We have decided that as your play was interrupted, you shall give it again – in Hall – before the entire school" (Louise said this slowly and impressively), "and as, of course, it would be a pity not to carry out your full arrangements, you will provide refreshments as before. You will have enough among your tuck."

At this awful pronouncement, the party began to babble wildly. To do them justice, it was not the loss of cakes and sweets that worried them at first. But to have to give that decidedly sketchy play before the whole school was more than they had bargained for. Their cup was brimmed when Louise blandly added, "And, by the way, all your so-called audience are to be fitted with parts."

Even Betty Wynne-Davies had never imagined anything quite so awful in the way of punishment, and lost her head accordingly.

"We won't do it!" she cried, shouting to make herself heard above the chorus of exclamations of horror. "We won't do it, and you can't make us!"

"Be silent!" said Louise, and her tone reduced the Middles to immediate silence.

The Head Girl looked at them. Then she said quietly, "There is one alternative, and one only. You will either do as I said, or you will each get a Head Mistress's report."

Checkmate!

No one – except, perhaps Betty, Elizabeth, and one or two others who were still under the impression that this dread punishment had been exaggerated to them – wanted a report. The old girls, in particular, would have raised fresh storms of protest if they had dared. As it was, they could only stand looking at the Head Girl in wide-eyed horror. Only Betty was inclined to stand up to her.

"And suppose we say we prefer that?" she demanded, all her native impudence showing in her voice, the tilt of her head, her whole attitude.

"That must be for *all* of you to decide," said Louise gravely. "I'll just add that the weekend after this is to be kept as half term. All girls with Headmistress's reports will not, of course, be allowed to go with the school to Salzburg."

That knocked all their props from under them. Not even Betty wanted to lose that tremendous treat. She stood back, all the cheekiness gone from her for the moment, and the prefects knew the battle was won. The play would be given somehow. And it was unlikely that, after this, any girl would lightly break dormitory rules again.

CHAPTER 5

Salzburg

The play was over. From the point of view of the audience, it had been a great success. The actors thought otherwise. When you have planned a tremendous tragedy, it is rather a shock to have it treated as a farce, and that was what the school had done about "The Duchess's Tragedy", written by Elizabeth Arnett.

The talented playwright herself had sulked for the rest of the week. She could see nothing to laugh about. But the fact remained that the school had sat through the show, holding its sides, and wiping its tears away.

Being nothing if not ambitious, Elizabeth had placed the scene in Spain – of which country she knew nothing – and had introduced the Duchess Mariquita, a beautiful young heiress, in the power of an unscrupulous guardian, Don Juan, who had resolved to force her to wed his son. Mariquita, unfortunately, was in love with a noble youth, Don Antonio, who adored her. Finding that her guardian meant to have his own way, she persuaded her lover to elope with her, and the pair were caught in the act by Don Juan. He forced the unlucky Antonio to fight a duel with his son, who, of course, killed his rival, whereupon the Duchess, snatching a small phial from the bosom of her dress, took poison and died.

Elizabeth had felt sure that this pathetic ending would bring down the house – and so it did, though not quite as she had imagined. Alixe dropped heavily on the "corpse" of her beloved, and Don Antonio, receiving the full force of his lady love's seven stone on his chest, gave vent to a complicated sound and doubled up his legs in a most uncorpselike manner. It had been impossible for anyone to

44

laugh any more just then; but Joey Bettany had slid off her chair with a sound as weird as Don Antonio's, and several senior Middles had collapsed on top of each other with hysterical groans.

Perhaps the proceedings would have been less riotous had it not been that, during the duel, Don Antonio felt the elastic in the top of his knickers give, and he had had to fight the last rounds holding up his nether garments, which rather marred the effect. That had been too much for even the staff. Miss Annersley wept gently; and Miss Edwards and Miss Nalder had to hold each other up.

However, it was all in the past now. Louise had wound up the affair with a brief but stern lecture on what would happen if plays were ever again given on the roof garden at unlawful hours; and the party involved in it had felt that, having made fools of themselves, as well as being deprived of all tuck for the rest of the term, they had better walk delicately for the next few weeks.

So the days passed, and at long last came the Friday with its glorious realization that work was ended for five days, and that morning they were off to Salzburg!

They were to go by coach, the staff preferring to keep their girls all under their own eyes. The Juniors went down to Innsbruck with their own staff and four of the prefects who had sacrificed themselves and given up the Salzburg trip. The Seniors were accompanied by all the rest of the resident staff, with the exception of Mesdemoiselles Lachenais and Berné, who were to spend the weekend at the Sonnalpe with Mademoiselle Lepâttre. Joey Bettany was coming, though, and with her, the Robin. They, and Paula von Rothenfels and her little sister Irma, would stay with Wanda von Glück, once Wanda von Eschenau, the loveliest girl who had ever been at the Chalet School, which had always had a good share of pretty girls.

Wanda had been married nearly four years now; and little Kurt, her small son, was just three; while a tiny sister had come to join him that April. Those of the girls who had known Wanda in her schooldays were looking forward to making acquaintance with Baby Maria Ileana, and Maria Marani, a very old friend, had complained bitterly because there would be no room for her.

"I remember Marie von Eschenau," remarked Hilary as she took her seat beside Gillian Linton. "I always thought her the loveliest thing I ever saw. I simply don't believe even her own sister could beat her!"

"Doubting Thomas!" mocked Gillian. "Why, Wanda might have stepped out of a fairytale. It's to be hoped little Maria Ileana takes after her. Friedel von Glück is quite passable, but he's no beauty."

"Wanda always was the beauty of our family," said Paula who was behind them. "It is strange that *we* should be so plain."

"Can't say I've ever noticed it particularly," said Hilary. "Oh, no one would stop to stare at you, but you're no worse than anyone else."

From the other side of the coach, Evadne Lannis broke into this with, "Say, Joey! D'you remember the *last* time we three were in Salzburg?"

"Rather!" said Jo, as she pulled the Robin down beside her. "Our hotel caught fire in the night."

"And that horrid, fat Frau Berlin was there and tried to rush down the fire escape after us!" chimed in the Robin.

"Remember what happened afterwards when Grizel tried to comb her hair?" asked Evadne. "Gee! That was a nasty shock!"

The coach, now full, began to move off as Hilary demanded, "Who is Grizel? And what did happen?"

"Grizel? She's Miss Cochrane up at the Annexe," said Evadne. "And her hair *came off*!"

"What? Do you mean she went bald?" gasped Hilary.

"Oh dear, no," explained Joey. "Only, she had long curls in those days, and they had got caught, and when she began combing, they simply came away. What a sight she looked!"

"Poppa nearly threw a fit," added Evadne. "He was in charge of us, you see, and I guess he thought Madame – she was still at school then – would think he'd been doing something out of sight for her to get like that. She had to go to the hairdresser's next morning, and get it properly cut. Joey, d'you remember how everyone yelled when we got back to school and they saw her?"

"They did yell, rather," agreed Jo. "No wonder, either!"

"And Grizel has never let it grow again," added the Robin. "Do you think she ever will?"

"Not she! She says it's a great saving of time – and so it is," said Jo, touching the flat plaits above her ears with a tentative hand.

"I don't know how it is," observed Cornelia Flower, "but you always seem up to the neck in adventures, Jo. If there *is* a chance of one, you're in it."

"Not always," retorted Jo. "I wasn't there when that madman carried you off to the salt caves. That was adventure enough for anyone."

Cornelia shivered. "Don't talk of it! I still have nightmares."

"We've had some adventurous times altogether at school," said Paula complacently.

"Too adventurous, sometimes," struck in Miss Wilson, who was sitting at the back with Betty Wynne-Davies and Biddy O'Ryan on either side of her. "Let's see if we can enjoy Salzburg without thrills of any kind for once. I haven't forgotten what happened when we took you girls to Oberammergau to see the Passion Play."

Those present who had been involved in that momentous affair went darkly red; and Evadne murmured to Cornelia that she thought it real mean of Bill to drag up a thing like that years after it had happened!

However, Miss Wilson was merciful, and turned the conversation by asking how many of those present had been to Salzburg before. Some of them had, and most of them knew something of its history. Evadne declared her intention of getting into the Franciscan church some day to hear the Pansymphonicon, the musical instrument invented by one of the friars.

"You cannot!" cried Paula. "No women are ever admitted!"

"Yes, and I think it's real mean of them," returned Evadne. "It's the only one of its kind in the world, and I'm bound to hear it before I die – if I have to crop my hair and wear boys' clothes to get in."

"You won't do it this time," said Miss Wilson firmly.

Evadne said no more. She knew better than to argue with Bill, who was past mistress in a certain form of sarcasm which, as its victims always declared, made you want to curl up and die. Equally, she knew that there was no hope of carrying out any mad plans when she was with a school party.

"I wish Momma and Poppa were at Salzburg now," she said, when she thought it safe to draw notice to herself again. "They needn't have gone off to New York just yet!"

"When will they be home?" asked Hilary. "What will you do about hols if they're still away, Evvy?"

"I'm going to Die Rosen," explained Evadne. "They're away till October, and the house is shut up with just Suzette in charge. I don't want to see Susie all that much, so I'm going to Madame."

It was not such a long drive to Salzburg that people were tired out when they arrived, although some of the younger girls were beginning to complain of having to sit still so long. But at last they began running along a road with quiet chalets and gay gardens on either side. A gleam of silver caught their eyes, and they knew they were looking at the Salzach, and were practically there. Twenty minutes later saw them climbing down from the coaches before the

48

Münchener Hof in the Dreifaltigkeitsgasse, and their journey was over.

"Not an incident to write home about!" Louise put in. "I reckon this is going to be a really peaceful half term for once."

"This is where we leave you," said Jo, as she rescued the suitcases containing her own and the Robin's possessions.

"How are you getting to Wanda's?" asked Miss Wilson. "You certainly can't walk to the other side of the town, you know."

"It's all right," said Jo placidly. "Wolfram von Eschenau is to meet us at the end of the street with the car, and will drive us up the Mönschberg."

"Did he know what time to expect you?"

"Yes, I rang them up just before we started, and he said he would meet us here. – He's there! That's the horn!" as a motor horn suddenly produced a violent fantasia which woke the echoes.

Miss Wilson laughed. "Very well. You can get off. We won't expect to see anything more of you today; but Paula and Irma, at any rate, must join us here by half-past nine tomorrow. Whether the Robin comes or not depends on you and Wanda. Use your common sense, Jo, and don't let her overdo things."

"I'll be careful," agreed Jo. "Good Heavens! Wolfram will burst that thing if he goes on like that much longer! – Come along, you people. – Goodbye, Miss Wilson! 'Bye, everyone!" Then she fled, followed by the other three, while Miss Wilson, having seen the last of her pupils into the pension, followed them to find out about rooms and other arrangements.

The four visitors to the Mönschberg, where Wanda von Glück lived, were met by her young brother, Wolfram von Eschenau, a handsome lad of seventeen or so, who welcomed them to the car.

"How is everyone, Wolfram?" asked Jo as he settled them.

"Very well," replied Wolfram, as he shut the door and sprang into the driver's seat. "Wanda is longing to see you all and to show you the little one. Father and mother are not at home just now. They have had to go to Styria to see to the affairs of our cousin Andreyev who has just died."

"Cousin Andreyev dead?" exclaimed Paula.

"A fortnight ago. A good thing, too," said Wolfram callously. "As it is, he has squandered almost all his inheritance. Father says that he expects there will be scarcely anything left, and the estate cannot be sold until Marco comes of age - which will not be for fourteen years."

"How many children are there?" asked Jo.

"Three - Anna, Wolferl, and Marco. Cousin Maria died when Marco was a baby, and Andreyev has made ducks and drakes, as you say, of everything since then."

"Poor little souls! Whatever will become of them?"

"Father and mother will care for them. They will send Anna to the Chalet School; and Wolferl goes to the Jesuiten in Wien. Marco is too small, and will live with us."

"Is that all the news?" demanded Paula, who had never known her cousin Andreyev personally, so was not grieved over his death.

"No. Our cousin Giannini is also appointed a guardian, and has had to go to Styria. He has left his twin children with Wanda, as his wife died recently, and he prefers not to leave them to aunts. Friedel can manage the boy; and the girl is in awe of Wanda at present. Such children you never saw! Well for them they are going to school in September! They need it!"

"What are their names?" asked Jo, suddenly suspicious.

"Maria and Mario di Balbini. Their father is Prince Balbini."

"I knew it!"

Wolfram slowed down, and turned to look at her. "You *knew* it? Pray how did you know it? I'm sure Marie has never named them to you, for we scarcely know them."

"We know because we've had some sweet experiences with them. Their final exploit was to kidnap young Sybil, and my sister was ill with the shock and worry. Do you mean to say they're with Wanda?"

"Yes, indeed. But you need not trouble yourself. Friedel can manage them. And if the *boy* worries you, I'll smack his head," replied Wolfram, whose English was almost perfect.

"Oh, I'm not bothering about that. Come to that, I can handle them myself. But it's rather a nuisance just now. I've heaps of things I want to discuss with Wanda."

"I'll keep them out of your way. Cheer up, Joey, and smile, for pity's sake! We are nearly there, and if Wanda sees you looking so melancholy she will think something is seriously wrong."

Joey pulled herself together, and produced a smile when Wanda, slight, graceful, and lovely as any fairy tale princess, swung herself up on the running board of the car two minutes later, and gave them an enthusiastic welcome.

"Oh, how delightful to have you all! I'm longing to see you and hear all the news! Quickly, to the house, Wolfram! We have so much to say, and there is Baby to show them!"

"Yes," said Jo, forgetting the Balbini twins for the moment. "How are the babies, Wanda? Is Maria Ileana like you or Friedel?"

"You, I hope, for her sake," put in Paula.

Wanda laughed. Then as Wolfram drew up before the door, she sprang down, and opened the car door. "You'll laugh when you see her; but she is like neither of us. She is the image of Wolfram, and he is ashamed of it, if you please! But she is a darling, and good as gold! Come along, all of you! Welcome to our home, and thrice welcome! Oh, Joey! How nice to have you again!"

She hurried them all into the salon where, guarded by a nurse in picturesque Tyrolean costume, were little Keferl, as small Kurt was called, and his tiny sister. The Balbini children were there, too, but no one noticed them for the moment.

"Here they are!" exclaimed Wanda, as her little son paddled across the room to grab her skirts and chuckle. "Hasn't Keferl grown? And this is our Blümchen – our little Maria Ileana!"

The girls kissed Keferl, and then bent over the baby. She was, as Jo said, one of the sweetest babies imaginable. The mop of hair that curled all over her head was flaxen-fair; her eyes were forget-me-not blue, and her little face like a wild rose; her feet and hands were the daintiest things you could see. Jo took her, and held her, examining her closely. Then she gave a glance to handsome Wolfram who was standing near, looking sheepish.

"Wanda's right, Wolfram!" she exclaimed. "There's only one funnier likeness, and that's Primula Mary Venables' likeness to Jem. I've always said she ought to be his daughter and not his niece! Oh, Wanda! What a little darling!"

"Isn't she?" said Wanda with fond pride. "And she is so good, Joey!"

"She is – or she'd be yelling with everyone thronging round her like this! Yes, Paula; you may have her. I must have a word with Keferl."

After twenty minutes of this, Wanda called the Balbini children, and bade them shake hands with her visitors. They did so shyly, but Jo was too kind to remind them of past scores. The young hostess then took off her friends and showed them their rooms.

"Paula and Irma are together," she said with a smile; "and I have put you and Robin here, Joey. You don't mind sleeping together, do you? I have had to make up the camp bed for Maria in the babies' room, or we should have taken them in with us, and given you that. But in the circumstances, this was the best I could do; and I could scarcely refuse Cousin Gian, especially when he is in such trouble."

"It's lovely, Wanda," said Jo, with an appreciative look round the dainty room which showed the careful mistress. Wanda von Glück had never known luxury, and, indeed, had it not been for the von Eschenau great-aunt from whom she had every one of her five baptismal names, the von Glücks would not have been so comfortable, since Friedel was a fourth son. But the old lady had left her namesake her own small fortune; so, while they had to be careful, they were able to enjoy a modest luxury. Happy Wanda never dreamt of envying her little sister her marriage with the wealthy young Baron von und zu Wertheimer. She and Friedel were ideally happy, and now their little daughter had come, asked for nothing further.

She said something of this when Paula and the children had run off, and Jo nodded. "Yes, it's easy to see that. And Gisela is happy as the day is long; and so is Bernhilda. Oh, by the way, I've some news for you! Bernie expects a new arrival in November. She said I might tell you."

"Oh, Joey! What delightful news!" exclaimed Wanda.

"Yes, they're all very thrilled about it."

"I don't wonder! Well, I only hope it's a little girl. Boys are always better if they have younger sisters to care for, I think. Now I must go and see to my other guests. Come down when you're ready. We shall be in the garden, I expect. The children live out there, this weather, and will do so as long as it's possible."

"Like our little crowd," agreed Jo. "Right! I'll just make myself fit to be seen, and then I'll join you. Don't let Rob run about too much, will you?"

"No. Besides, there will be lemonade and cakes under the lindens in a few minutes," called Wanda from the stairs. "Be quick, Jo!"

That was the beginning of a delightful weekend, into which they crammed as much sightseeing as possible, and enjoyed themselves immensely. Robin was not allowed to do much; but she was quite happy to stay in the shady

53

garden and play with the von Glück babies, while the others explored Salzburg and its surroundings as thoroughly as they could. They saw the Mozart Museum with the various relics of the great master, and thrilled to the story of his life, first in the little, quiet city on the banks of the Salzach; then travelling with his sister, Nanerl, and meeting all the great ones of the day; his young manhood, so filled with disappointments and rebuffs; his marriage; his days of poverty in Vienna, where he had been loudly hailed as a child prodigy; and finally his death, with its queer foreshadowing of the Requiem Mass which was his final work; his pauper's funeral; and now his fame.

"I think I'll write a novel about it some day," said Joey.

"Oh, do, Joey!" cried Gillian. "It would make a glorious novel!"

"Jo would have her work cut out," said Miss Stewart, who was with them. "I should think it would mean study for two or three years beforehand, Jo. There is so much documentary evidence of those times, and, whatever else you are, for pity's sake be accurate in your history!"

Jo chuckled. "Don't worry. It's only an idea."

"Well, suppose you leave ideas alone and come for Mittagessen now," proposed Miss Wilson, who had been listening with amusement.

"Where are we feeding?" asked Jo.

"St Peter's Stiftkeller. It's quite famous, and you ought to be able to say that you've had a meal there," explained Miss Stewart.

"Why is it famous?" asked Evadne. "Were there any murders there?"

"Don't be so bloodthirsty!" Miss Stewart reproved her. "It's famous because it's part of St Peter's Abbey, which was founded by St Rupert in 696, and which was the real foundation of Salzburg. The town grew up round the abbey like many other towns – our own Bury St Edmunds, for instance. After Mittagessen, we'll go and see the abbey itself. Quite a lot of it is open to visitors – including the library, Jo.''

"Oh, good!" exclaimed Jo. "So often a monastery library is in the Enclosure, and then outsiders can't get even a sniff at it. This is rather a famous one, isn't it?"

"It is. They have over seventy thousand books, besides manuscripts. So for once you may see enough books to suit you!"

"What richness!" And Jo heaved a sigh of rapture.

The next night they went to the Opera House to hear one of Mozart's operas, "Die Zauberflöte", and they enjoyed it enormously. The last day was given up to a visit to Hellbrunn, the place which Archbishop Wolf Dietrich built for Salome Alt. Wolf Dietrich might not have been all he ought as Archbishop; but there is no doubt that he could build. Hellbrunn, with its lovely garden, fountains, statues, and exquisite house, is a treasure of which the Salzburgers are very proud.

The tremendous heat made the coolness of the out-of-doors under the great trees very refreshing, and they had a day which, as Louise said, they would never forget.

"It's been a glorious half term," said Joey, as she and the other three hung out of Wolfram's car to say goodbye to the rest. "For once in a way we've had no troubles; and even the Middles have behaved like sane beings!"

A murmur of indignation at this insult arose from the Middles. But Gillian Linton shook her head. "We aren't back yet," she said warningly. "Don't crow too soon, Jo."

Jo opened her eyes. "Why, what on earth *could* happen now? We have to pack tonight, and tomorrow the coaches come for us at ten o'clock. Even *Middles* couldn't achieve much in the way of wickedness now."

"You never can tell," said Louise who was standing near. "However, I agree with Jo. I don't see what harm can come now. And it's been a really delightful rest after all the alarums and excursions we've had this term."

55

However, neither Jo nor Louise was cut out for a prophetess, and before they reached the Tiernsee, some of them were to have such an adventure as was to cause the younger ones nightmares and also add to the white hairs the staff already possessed. Finally, it was to give Jo an exciting scene for her new book, though that is rather beside the mark, and, as she said later, was far from necessary.

CHAPTER 6

A Hair-Raising Adventure

Ten o'clock on the next day came all too soon for most folk, though the staff were not exactly sorry. As Miss Wilson observed to Miss Stewart, the responsibility of a hundred or so girls was no joke.

"Well, it's practically over now," said Miss Stewart soothingly. "Nothing can happen now – unless we crash into anything on the road, and that's not likely. We go by quiet ways, and the drivers are good. Don't worry, my dear. You'll only give yourself wrinkles to no good purpose."

"I'm thankful we've had such glorious weather," said Miss Wilson, glancing up at the sky as she spoke. "Unless I'm much mistaken, we're in for a downpour today. Just look at that sky!"

Miss Stewart glanced at it. "Oh, well, it won't hurt us. We shall be under cover. Besides, we may run out of it. Lots of these storms are merely local, you know."

"I know. But they prophesized thunder for all the Tyrol over the radio last night, so I shan't be surprised if we catch it. Hello! The girls are all in. Come along, you people!"

She watched the rest of the staff – Miss Annersley was not with them, having elected to spend her half term at the Sonnalpe – taking their seats, and then swung herself into the last of the coaches where Miss Stewart was already sitting, and went to where Joey, Paula, Louise, Gillian, and Hilary had the back seat.

"Room for a little one?" she smiled.

"Yes, if you don't mind a crush," said Jo, moving up. "Shove along, Lulu. You don't want the whole seat, do you?"

"Don't be so rude!" retorted Louise, moving along as

she spoke. "Is that all right, Miss Wilson? It isn't such a crush as when we came, thanks to Herr von Glück taking Robin and Irma back with him, but we're pretty tightly packed even so."

"Those big boxes of souvenirs you all insisted on buying take up so much room," said Miss Wilson. "I hope I'm not crowding anyone?"

"Not in the least – we're quite comfortable!" they chorused.

The coach had started now, and they were moving through the streets that looked so dark under the heavy sky.

"What a difference sunlight makes," said Jo involuntarily. "It looks as though we are in for a storm, doesn't it?"

"Yes; but it won't hurt us with all the rubber there is about us," said Gillian. "Hello! Another stop! We shall get out of Salzburg some time at this rate!"

"Look at the Salzach!" cried Hilary. "It's nearly *black* today!"

They looked out of the windows at the river, which seemed to flow in a peculiarly sluggish way. The silver of its waters was gone, and it had a threatening, sullen look.

"I'm glad the two babes went with Friedel," said Jo. "If we run into a storm we may get hung up. In the train they'll be all right, though. What a good thing the firm wanted Friedel to go to Innsbruck today!"

Miss Wilson agreed fervently, and then turned the conversation, and they chatted about all they had seen at Salzburg. Quick chaff passed among them, and the coach rang with their laughter. At noon they stopped by the wayside to eat the Mittagessen put up for them by the pension people. The rain had not yet come, though the lowering sky promised something unusual in the way of storms when it began. Miss Wilson unpacked the baskets, exclaiming at the quantities of food supplied.

"Good gracious! What an impression our appetites must

have made on them!'' she cried.

"But isn't that for another meal in the afternoon as well?'' asked Jo.

"Oh, no! Those boxes under the seat hold Kuchen and Brödchen and thermos flasks of hot coffee. This is all intended for Mittagessen.''

"Then I should say you have all behaved most greedily.''

"Indeed we didn't!'' cried Gillian indignantly. "Don't be so horrid, Jo!''

"I'm only judging by what they've packed for us. Oh, well, it'll never come wrong! We probably shan't get home till late, and we may be thankful of a snack towards evening.''

The meal ended, for Miss Wilson and Miss Stewart would permit of no dawdling with that sky before their eyes, and they packed up the bountiful remains of the feast and climbed back into the coach.

"And just in time,'' said Jo as she glanced out of the window. "I wonder if the others have caught it? What a nuisance we got so far left behind with those traffic jams!''

She glanced again at the window, where big splashes of rain were forming. Ten minutes later, the panes were hidden beneath veils of streaming water through which it was impossible to see, and the noise the rain made dancing on the thin rubber sheet which had been tied over the roof defies description.

"I don't see how the driver can see his way at all,'' said Hilary.

"Oh, he has a double windscreen wiper,'' replied Louise comfortably.

However, it was soon plain that even the double windscreen wiper was no use in this torrent. The driver switched it off in the hope that the very force of the rain would wash the windscreen clear; but his hope was vain. For about an hour he crawled along, afraid to risk any sort of speed for they were now among the mountains and, though the road was a good one, parts of it ran along the banks of streams which must be flooded by all this rain, and he had no wish for an accident.

Then they came to a place where the river had flooded the road to a depth of twelve or fifteen inches, and it was plain that, further on, the water was even deeper. He put the bus into reverse and began to back slowly along the road he had come. The girls thought it fun, and took it as a joke, laughing over it and making all sort of lurid prophecies. The mistresses, however, remained silent, and soon the Seniors began to grasp that those in charge felt uneasy, and fell silent, too. However, the Middles more than made up for that. Some of the very rowdiest of the clan were in this coach, and they were excited by the holiday and this wholly unexpected sort of journey.

"P'raps we'll have to stay out all night," giggled Elizabeth Arnett.

"P'raps the bus'll overturn and we'll have to get out and walk," contributed Betty Wynne-Davies.

"Swim, don't you mean?" demanded Jeanne le Cadoulec, a Breton girl of about fifteen. "I do not think one could walk far among so much water."

"What a noise the wind makes!" shivered Violet Allison, the Five B prefect. "I do hate it when it moans like that!"

"Oh, that's only because it's raining so," said Ruth Wynyard, a jolly, tomboyish person of fourteen. "Don't be so silly, Vi!"

The merry chatter went on, and the driver of the coach presently added to the merriment by switching on the radio as well as the light. He was still backing slowly, and with much consultation of his mate, for it was clear that the whole of this path would shortly be well under water. He wanted to get back to the fork, which would mean a long way round for them, but no driving through agitated rivers. Unfortunately, the road was too narrow to allow turning, and wound so much that backing had to be done very slowly and carefully. On the one hand was the river, which, even here, was beginning to send little trickles of water across the way. On the other was the mountain wall, which rose sheerly for some thirty or forty feet just there.

Slowly, slowly, the great coach moved backwards, almost a foot at a time. The driver knew that presently he must come to a slight dip, and here he would have water again to negotiate. But if he could get safely past this, the road rose gradually all the way to the fork, and there need be no further trouble about floods. A cry from his mate warned him that the dip was at hand, and he drove even more cautiously.

"How much further are we going to back?" demanded Jo suddenly.

"I don't know," said Miss Stewart from her seat a little way up the aisle. "Hello! We're going through water again! Listen to that!"

The girls listened, and heard, above the noise of the rain and wind, the unmistakable "Sh-sh-sh-sh!" of wheels going through water.

"I wonder if it is very deep?" said Jeanne suddenly. "It sounds like it."

"Oh, not more than an inch or two," replied Jo airily, though she felt sure that she was understating it. Judging by the sound there was a good deal more than an inch or two. However, Jenne was easily satisfied, and she turned back to listen to Betty and Elizabeth, who were telling tall stories of motoring experiences against each other. They were hushed next moment by a low growl of thunder in the distance.

"Thunder!" gasped Alixe von Elsen, who had a nervous dread of it.

"What of it?" asked Gillian quickly, for Alixe's tones were shaking.

"It's a good distance off, anyway," added Louise soothingly.

The next moment, she and the rest jumped violently, for there came a second peal, considerably nearer.

"It's travelling fast," said Miss Wilson. "Better have the radio switched off, I think. Emmie, tap on the glass and ask the driver to turn it off, will you?"

Emmie did as she was told, and the driver took enough time from his anxious negotiation of the road to switch the radio off.

At long last they were out of the dip, and, now that they were above the water and on a fairly straight stretch of road, the driver quickened his speed a little. If only the storm would hold up until he could swing the coach into the longer way, all would be well. But the storm had no idea of being so obliging. It came up with appalling rapidity, and long before they reached the fork it was on them.

Those who have experienced a thunderstorm in mountainous country will realize something of that one. The thunder crashed and pealed among the heights, re-echoing and reverberating till it seemed as though it never ceased for a moment. The flashes of lightning cut across the black sky or danced madly down the mountainside almost without cessation, and the rain was worse than ever. The driver's mate had run for cover, and the driver had stopped the bus, though he kept his engine just ticking over so as to be ready to start again as soon as possible.

Anxiously he listened to it, and calculated whether he had enough petrol to get them to the next filling station. No more than the two mistresses did he want to be stranded overnight among the mountains with a rising river – *several* rising rivers, so far as that went – and a load of schoolgirls who might be expected to become hysterical. He was agreeably surprised that it had not happened so far.

In the coach, the girls sat almost silent. Some of them were badly frightened, despite Gillian's assurance. Some of them were awed by the magnificence of the storm. Alixe was trying to control herself, and Jo was keeping a watchful eye on her. Presently, in a momentary silence, she called, "Alixe, come here!"

Alixe turned a white face to her. 'I am afraid!" she jerked out.

Joey got up and marched down the aisle. "Come along," she said. "You can sit on my knee for a little."

Gillian had gone to join her own younger sister, Joyce, who was also nervous of thunder. Joey put Alixe in her place, and put an arm round the child. Alixe hid her eyes against the elder girl's shoulder, and lay still. At each peal of thunder, shivers went through her, but they could help her no further at present.

The driver pulled back the glass slide between his little cabin and the main body, and asked Emmie Linders to tell the others to draw the curtains. "So will you shut out the lightning," he said, "and it will be better. We can but wait. When the storm ends, I will drive as fast as I can by the long route. But until then we must remain where we are."

Emmie did as he told her, and certainly, when the thick, dark green curtains had been drawn, things looked more cheerful. Mercifully, the batteries were all right, and the bright glow of the electric light was comforting.

Presently, Miss Wilson looked at her watch. "Half-past four! Time for Kaffee und Kuchen! Pull out the boxes, girls, and we'll have a meal. We'll feel better then." Such of them as were not too scared to move did as she bade them. The pension people had packed piles of delicious cakes and Brödchen, and the coffee in the big flasks was steaming hot. Miss Wilson proved quite right. When they had had a good meal, most of them felt better, even though the storm was still raging awesomely in the narrow pass.

When she had finished, Miss Wilson turned Emmie Linders and her partner, Elsa Fischer, out of their seat, and pushing back the glass slide, offered the men in the little cabin coffee and cakes, which they accepted thankfully. She remained chatting with them till they had finished. Then she closed the slide once more, and came back to her own place, Emmie and Elsa taking theirs.

Miss Stewart, who had joined the back seat crowd, looked anxiously at her colleague. Something in the steady grey eyes told her that all was not well. Miss Wilson sat down, and began to speak to her in rapid if not always correct Italian. The driver did not fear the lightning; nor did he think the river likely to bother them, though it was certainly rising rapidly. But he was doubtful if he had enough petrol to get them to the next filling station.

"And if that is the case," concluded Miss Wilson, "we may be stranded on the road all night. There certainly won't be any cars abroad in this weather."

"Well, thank Heaven this is July and dawn comes early!" replied Miss Stewart fervently.

Joey knew Italian – the only one of the girls there who could follow Bill – and her eyes widened as she took in the news. She shifted Alixe a little, and addressed Miss Wilson in Italian as fluent and a good deal more grammatical. "Are we really likely to have to spend the night out?"

"Oh, I forgot *you* spoke Italian," said Miss Wilson. "Yes, it begins to look like it."

"What a mess! I wonder where the others are, or if they got through."

"They would be able to get to the next village, I think," said Miss Wilson. "If we hadn't been so delayed by those traffic jams, we should have got through, too. As it is, I'm afraid we must just make the best of things."

"What a nuisance it is! Oh, well, I suppose it might have been worse. We might have had the babes with us."

"Yes, I'm thankful we're saved that," said Miss Wilson emphatically.

An interruption came at that moment from Emmie Linders. Would Miss Wilson please go and speak to the driver? Bill got up and went to him. She bundled Emmie and Elsa out of their places once more, and opening the slide, leaned forward. As she did so, she caught her breath with a sudden gasp. The driver had switched on his headlights, and their reflection gleamed back from water only three feet beyond the coach.

"You see, Fräulein?" said the man, forgetting courtesy in his anxiety, and addressing her by the familiar second person instead of the more mannerly third. "The river rises faster than I feared. Before long it will flow round us, and I do not know how high it may rise."

"What can we do?" asked Miss Wilson anxiously.

"I will try to back a little more. But I dare not go far, for there is a bad bend not far from here, and at present I could not risk it. Also, the wind rises, and, while we are protected here, round the bend we should get its full force, and that might make the coach rock, heavy as it is, which would alarm the young ladies.".

"Do you think the river will rise much more?"

"I cannot tell. Such a storm as this I have never known before. Das Fräulein will understand that there are many little streams, and all are swollen. All run into the river, and it is impossible to say what it will do."

"It is all uphill, is it not?" queried the worried mistress.

"Oh, yes. The further back, the steeper, also. Hans, here, will descend and guide me; and perhaps das Fräulein would be so good as to permit him a cup of coffee when he returns?"

"Of course," said Miss Wilson. "Wait! I have a long india rubber cloak which he can throw round him. It will save him from getting so wet."

She went back and got the cloak from her suitcase. Hans flung it over his head with a word of grateful thanks, and then dropped down into the wet road. Presently, above the crashing of the thunder and the howling of the wind, they could hear his voice, and the driver began his cautious reversing again.

The movement of the coach, unexpected by most of the girls, startled them into eager questions, and even Alixe sat up to enquire what was happening.

"We are backing further up the road," said Miss Wilson.

"Shall we be getting on now?" asked Gillian wistfully.

"You know as much as I do, Gillian. We certainly shall if it's possible. I don't suppose those men want to camp out here for the night any more than we do."

However, when the coach had been backed a good thirty yards or so, the driver shut off his engine. He could do no more. He felt certain that his petrol would never get them to the next filling station. But he hoped that they were now well out of reach of the river, since, at this part, the road sloped steeply. But he had a new worry. Would his brakes hold? The rain was making the road surface slippery, and the coach was heavy. Dared he trust the brakes alone?

On consideration he decided that he dared not. The wheels must be wedged. He was responsible for the safety of his passengers, and he dared run no risks. With a groan for the weather, he fastened up his coat and swung himself to the ground, where he was met by his mate.

"We must wedge the wheels with stones," he told him. "I dare not risk the brakes."

Hans glanced round. Some moderate-sized boulders were at hand, and the two men, with grunts and much effort, contrived to wedge them against the wheels, thus making the coach as secure as possible. But when that was done, they had done all they could. The only course left to them was to stay where they were till dawn, when they must hope that some car or lorry would pass from which they could get petrol, and so continue their journey.

The driver told Miss Wilson all this when she passed cups of steaming coffee from a fresh flask through the slide to them. He assured her of the safety of the coach. Short of an earthquake, it was unlikely to move. They were well above the river here, and he did not think the water could even wash the wheels. If it did, that would be all.

It was comparatively cheering news – but only comparatively. The idea of keeping twenty-two girls out there

66

all night with no proper beds for them was quite enough to turn the hair of any conscientious mistress grey. Miss Wilson withdrew to the back of the coach to tell Miss Stewart the latest and to consult with her as to what they should do. Needless to state, Joey joined in.

"What shall we do for beds?" she enquired.

"Manage with what we've got. And don't yell, Jo! Some of the children learn Italian, remember; and though I doubt if they can follow us, still, they might pick up ideas, and I don't want that."

"Sorry!" said Jo, quite impenitent. "Gill and the rest have picked up quite a few ideas already, though."

"Well, there's one blessing," said the ever-optimistic Miss Stewart.

"*I* can't see any!" snapped Miss Wilson.

"Pull yourself together, my child. We have plenty of food, and we might very well have had none. As it is, no one need starve. Look here, what time is it?"

Miss Wilson looked at her watch. "Half-past seven."

"Then what about a meal? When the girls have finished, tell them what's happened, and that we can't hope for rescue till the morning. Some of them are sleepy already – the atmosphere, I suppose. They'll take it as a joke – one does at their age! We've plenty of suitcases, thanks to having offered to fetch the first coach's cases. We'll fill in the spaces between the seats with them, and bed the children down that way. They can't take cold, for they'll be packed pretty tightly together. It won't be very comfortable, but it'll be better than letting them sleep sitting up. We can have the lights out, for I've got my torch, and I suppose you have yours—"

"And I've got mine," put in Jo eagerly.

"Good! Then we can save on the batteries of the coach. And this storm isn't going to last forever. The thunder's not nearly so loud now."

Bill's face relaxed. "That's true. And the peals aren't so

frequent, either. Well, I suppose it's the only thing to do. I'll tell the men, and you and Joey can spread the meal. After we've had that, everyone can go to bed, and we'll have those lights out. I've been wondering how long the batteries would last out."

She went back to confer with the men, while Joey and Miss Stewart, aided by Louise, Gillian, Paula, and Hilary, got ready a meal, and saw to it that everyone made a good one. Even when they had all finished and the men had been given a share, there was enough left for a frugal Frühstück in the morning, though most of the coffee was done.

"However, we shan't lack for *water*," said Jo cheerfully; "and I've got my travelling Etna with me. If only we had some tea or coffee we could manage nicely."

"We haven't either," said Miss Stewart briskly, "but you aren't much of a Guide, Jo, if you can't rise to a simple emergency of *that* kind." She raised her voice. "Will every girl please give me any stick chocolate she may have."

The girls looked puzzled. However, things were so odd, that this request made little difference to them. They handed over all stick or block chocolate quite cheerfully. Elizabeth and Betty contributed about two kilos between them, and went red when the mistress raised her eyebrows at the great lumps.

"You evidently didn't intend to starve," she said drily. 'I wonder how soon Matron would have been called to your assistance?"

The pair went back to their seats feeling rather silly, and Miss Stewart made haste to take the remainder, and piled it into a spare cardboard box. Then Miss Wilson ordered them to clear away all papers and put everything tidy.

"Make haste!" she said. "You won't hear anything until this bus is spick and span!"

They hastened to obey, and, when at length everything was "shipshape and Bristol fashion" and they were all sitting in their seats again, she stood up, smiling.

"Now!" she said.

CHAPTER 7

A Queer Night

"Girls," said Miss Wilson. "We're in for an adventure!"

A chorus of "Oo-ooh's!" ecstatic or otherwise according to the feelings of the speakers greeted this announcement.

"How, Miss Wilson?" asked Joyce Linton.

"We have to stay here all night."

"*All night?* But how can we?"

"There isn't a hotel anywhere – I know we didn't pass one!"

"Aber, Fräulein—"

"Mais, Mademoiselle—"

She held up a hand, and they quieted at once. "We must stay here, and when I say 'here', I mean in the coach," she told them. "There is water over the road – deep water. We can't turn back, because it is too dark to see and there is a dangerous turning just behind us. There is certainly no hotel near, or I might think of getting out and walking there, even in this rain. However, I think we can manage comfortably."

"And it won't be any worse than camping," added Jo unexpectedly.

"How shall we manage, Miss Wilson?" asked Gillian.

"Build up the suitcases between the seats to make them wide enough to take two people each. It will be rather like herrings in a box, but it won't hurt you for once. There are plenty of rugs, so you will be warm enough."

"But we won't be able to stretch," complained Elizabeth.

"You can manage for once," returned Miss Wilson inflexibly. "And in any case, it will be worse for the Seniors than for shrimps like you. Now we'll begin. Alixe and Elsa, out into the aisle. Hilary and Gillian, go and build up the suitcases."

The fun began. Seat by seat the spaces were built in, and the girls were tucked in on them, with one rug under each pair, and another over. It was not really cold, though the mistresses expected that as the night went on it might become so. Still, the girls would be so closely packed they would not feel it.

The "beds" were decidedly short, and it was difficult for some of the longer-legged people to settle in comfortably. However, at last they were all squeezed in except the Seniors on the back seat, and they were a real puzzle.

"It's lucky we offered to bring so many suitcases because we had some free seats," said Jo as she tucked in Alixe and Elsa for the fourth time. "Now, you two, if you wriggle uncovered again you may *stay* uncovered. That's the last time I'm bothering to tuck you up, so lie still!"

"I wish we knew what we can do for you people," said Miss Wilson, looking at the four big girls in perplexity.

"Three can lie on the seat if we enlarge it," suggested Joey. "What the rest of us can do, I don't know. It's worse than that night we were stuck in the Alpenhütte on the Stubai – remember, Miss Wilson?"

"I still get rheumatism in my foot where the bone was broken when there's bad weather about," admitted Miss Wilson.

"Couldn't we lie on the floor?" suggested Hilary.

"And catch cold from floor draughts? No thank you, Hilary! I'd rather be excused *that* addition to our adventures."

"Let's get the back seat built up first, and then we'll see," said Miss Stewart. "Come along, you folk. Bring the cases along."

They brought the last of the cases, and built up the back seat. Then Paula, Gillian, and Louise were fitted in, heads to tails, and discovered that if they lay quietly, Hilary could be managed too.

"Very well," said Miss Wilson. "Now, is that all right? You're sure you can manage?"

"Easily!" said Hilary, inwardly wondering how she would ever sleep, squeezed into that narrow space.

"You all right, Louise – Paula – Gillian?"

"Yes, thank you," cheerfully replied three drowsy voices.

"Then remember, girls, no more talking," warned Miss Wilson. "You are to try to go to sleep. Otherwise, you'll have to go straight to bed when we get back, and then you won't be able to tell your adventures to the others for another day."

That settled it, as she had known it would. Already three or four people had been thinking out the exciting stories they would have to tell, and to be forced to leave them for a whole day was not to be borne. The giggling and whispering died away almost at once, and the coach was quiet.

"I wonder if it's still raining so badly?" murmured Miss Stewart as she leaned up against the back of the seat on which Biddy O'Ryan and Mary Shaw were already sleeping as soundly as if they were safe in their own beds at St Clare's.

"The thunder's dying away," replied Miss Wilson from a similar position further down the coach.

Joey stretched across Cornelia and Evadne, who were almost asleep, and pulled aside a curtain to look out. Naturally, she could see nothing, but in the stillness it was plain that the rain was not quite so heavy, though it still came down steadily. "It's raining all right," she said as she let the curtain drop.

"The wind has veered a little," decided Miss Wilson, who had been listening carefully. "It's more on that side. Why do you want to know?"

"Because I do think we ought to try to open one or two of the windows, if it's only an inch or so. You could cut the

71

atmosphere with a knife, and it's bad for the girls to be sleeping in it," replied Miss Stewart.

"I know," said Miss Wilson. "On the other hand, if they get wet, we shall have a fine crop of colds for the end of term. I've been trying to decide which would be the worse, and I can't make up my mind."

"Risk the colds. *I* should," advised Joey, who was beginning to have a bad headache. "They'll all have frightful heads tomorrow otherwise."

Miss Wilson listened again. 'I think I will," she said, in the low tones in which they had all been speaking. "Con, you're the tallest. Can you stretch across and lower a window on that side without disturbing anyone? I think the girls are mostly asleep."

Miss Stewart nodded. "I can try, at any rate. Hold me, Nell, in case I slip, and I'll have a shot."

"Take this last case and stand on it," suggested Jo. "You'll get more purchase then."

Miss Stewart adopted the suggestion, and contrived to stretch across Emmie Linders and Thyra Eriksen and turn the handle which lowered the centre window, without rousing them. She opened the upper sash a bare two inches, but the relief in the atmosphere was at once apparent.

"I believe the wind will come right round," said Miss Wilson when she was once more back in her place. "In that case it may blow the rain off. I hope so, I'm sure."

"What time is it?" asked Jo, suppressing a yawn with difficulty.

Miss Stewart consulted her watch. "I make it just half-past ten."

"Only that? I thought it must be long after midnight!"

"No, I'm afraid we've a long vigil before us. But I see no reason why we should stand like this all the time," said Miss Wilson, severely practical. "We have this last suitcase and two rugs. Surely we can manage to make ourselves more comfortable. Let's see what we can do, and then I'll go along and ask the men to switch off the lights."

"Suppose one of us sits on the suitcase and the other two lay the rug on the floor and lie down," suggested Miss Stewart. "That ought to be a fairly efficient shield from floor draughts. Then I have my big ulster. Whoever sits on the case could tuck up in that, the two on the floor could have the other rug over them. It won't be ideal, but it will certainly be better than standing."

They experimented and found that she was right. Miss Wilson insisted that, as head of the party, she should have the case and coat, while Joey and Miss Stewart shared the two rugs on the floor. She left them to get settled, and passed down what was left of the aisle, having more than one narrow escape of falling over feet stuck out from the ends of the impromptu beds. As she said later on in the privacy of the staff room, the days of small feet seem gone for ever.

"Such *hoofs* as the girls showed I never expected to see! The majority of them must take sevens and eights! And I'm convinced some of them produced a foot or two extra just to trip me up. It was worse than crossing a glacier!"

"Can't say I noticed it," said Miss Stewart. "I'd no idea so many of the girls *snored*, though. Matey, I advise you to call in Dr Jem and have a hunt for adenoids. If anyone had passed, he must have thought the coach contained a nice selection of young lions, or a small herd of pigs!"

However, all this was later. At the time, Bill contrived to steer a steady course to the glass slide, which she opened, to find the two men drowsing contentedly in the cabin under a huge tarpaulin. The thunder was practically out of hearing now, though far away the lightning still flickered at intervals.

"The storm is passing," she said softly to the driver as he roused up. "We should be able to get off at dawn. Meanwhile, we have arranged for the young ladies to lie down and sleep, and we think perhaps it would be better if the lights were turned off. You have your sidelights and rearlights going, haven't you?"

He nodded. "Ja, gnädiges Fräulein. It is a good thought, and will save the batteries, though I would leave the lights on if das Fräulein so wishes. I would not have the young ladies frightened, poor little ones! They are brave as lions. I had feared they would all weep."

Miss Wilson suppressed a grin at the thought of some of her lambs weeping. They might grumble or become fractious, but tears were not in their line. She thanked the man for his consideration, but insisted that the girls would sleep better in the darkness.

"Give me time to get back to my seat," she said, "and then switch off the lights, please. We have torches if we need them."

He nodded his comprehension, and Miss Wilson contrived to return to her case without rousing anyone. She found Joey and Miss Stewart already stretched out, with one rug double beneath them, and the other tucked round them. They had unearthed sweaters and cardigans from their cases, and had rolled them up to form pillows, leaving one for Bill. She thanked them for their thoughtfulness; got into Miss Stewart's big ulster, pinning it firmly round her with safety pins, since she was a much slighter woman; tucked the "pillow" between her shoulders and the side of the seat against which she was leaning, and so prepared to make what she could of the night. At that moment the lights went out, for the driver had been watching her, and the bus was in darkness.

Miss Stewart soon dozed off. Miss Wilson, worried by her heavy responsibilities, and Joey, sensitive and impressionable, remained awake. Neither dared move for fear of waking anyone else, so neither knew that she was not alone in her wakefulness.

It was an eerie situation. Miss Wilson felt that she would have been thankful to be quit of it. Leaning against the side

74

of the seat, she gave herself up to pondering arrangements for the next morning. They must back out of the present path, of course. It was certainly flooded to some depth further on, and they could not hope to get through. Then they must go as far along the other way as their petrol would take them, and hope for a passing car or vehicle which could supply them with enough to get them to the nearest filling station.

Should she tell the man to drive to the nearest railway station and get the first train to Spärtz? She thought it over and then decided against it. Apart from anything else, she could imagine what the girls would look like after a night in the present circumstances, and that would be no good advertisement for the school. They must just go straight on. As soon as they came to an inn they must stop, and the girls could have a wash and brush-up, so that they might reach the Tiernthal looking as respectable as possible.

As she reached this point in her thoughts, there came a muttering from one end of the coach, and she jumped. Then she realized that it was only someone – probably Alixe – talking in her sleep, and sat back again. But her movement had told Jo that she was awake, and Joey murmured her name.

"I say! Bill!"

"Yes? Speak very low, Joey. I want these people to sleep until we get off again, if that's possible."

"Better pray the thunder doesn't return again, then," said Joey, *sotto voce*. "What I wanted to say is, what are we to do if Alixe tries to walk in her sleep after all this excitement?"

"She couldn't get far, at any rate," said Miss Wilson, wisely keeping the talk on a light plane, for she knew her Jo. "Besides, she's far too tired to do such a thing. No need to worry about that, Jo."

Moving cautiously, Jo wriggled free of her wrappings and stood up. "I say, Bill, switch on your torch a moment, will you? I don't want to wake up anyone by falling over her."

"You ought to be asleep," said Miss Wilson, nevertheless complying with the request. "You'll be half-dead tomorrow, you known."

"Can't sleep," said Jo laconically. "Oh, I'll have to spend tomorrow in bed, I suppose – or as much of it as is left after we get back. Shift up, and let me sit beside you a moment."

Miss Wilson moved, and Jo dropped down beside her. "What an experience we are having! This beats the Alpenhütte into a cocked hat!"

"For some things – not others," replied Bill, casting a thought to the agonizing pain she had undergone on that occasion. She had had a fall and broken a small bone in her foot, and her sufferings had been severe, though she had stoically said nothing about them.

Jo understood. "It was a bad time for you. Mercy! What's that?" she added in different tones.

"Only someone snoring, though I admit the sounds are rather hair-raising, especially heard under these conditions," replied Miss Wilson with a low laugh. Then she examined the illuminated dial of her watch. "Half-past midnight. The dawn comes about three. I wonder how soon we shall be able to get on our way again?"

"Not much before four, if then," said Joey. "It won't be light very early here; the mountains close it in so. I say! Someone is evidently giving us imitations of a wairus! Who on earth is it?"

"Don't you try to explore, for I won't have it. You'd only end by falling over someone and rousing the entire crowd. Look here, Joey, go back and lie down again. Close your eyes and count sheep jumping through a gap, and you'll soon get to sleep."

"It would be the first time if I did, Bill. *That* never made me sleep yet. Give me time to lie down again, then you can switch off your torch. Otherwise, we'll be rousing Charlie."

"Jo, it's disgraceful the way you call us Bill and Charlie! You might have some respect for our position if you have none for our age."

Jo chuckled under her breath. "How much older *are* you? Not many years, I fancy. D'you know, Bill, it's a queer thing, but since I've left school, you people seem to be getting years nearer my own age."

Miss Wilson laughed. "I'm thirty, if you really want to know. And Con is two years younger."

"Well, goodnight, Bill!"

"Goodnight, Jo. And if you *must* be familiar, I'd rather you made it my Christian name. There's no reason why you shouldn't now – so long as you don't do it before the other girls."

"Is it likely? But I didn't mean anything, you know?"

"I know that quite well. You're a cheeky child, Jo, but you're never impudent. Now do settle down and try to sleep."

"Oh, all right. I'll do my best."

Jo cautiously squirmed back to her place beside Miss Stewart, who never stirred, and Miss Wilson switched off her torch and closed her own eyes in a valiant effort to woo slumber. She must have been successful, for when next she was conscious of anything, it was that the steady pattering of the rain against the windows had ceased, and a faint grey light was stealing into the coach through the uncurtained end windows. She sat up, feeling very stiff and uncomfortable, and rather shivery. The girls were still sleeping, and so were Miss Stewart and Jo.

Miss Wilson got to her feet, and stretched till she felt better. Then she moved carefully down the coach to see that the girls were well covered up. Everyone must have slept like the dead, as she informed them some hours later, for even normally restless people did not seem to have stirred.

77

She glanced into the cabin, but the two men were sleeping as peacefully as the girls. Then she drew one of the curtains and looked out. The rain had stopped, but the road was very wet. She would have been thankful for a hot drink, but she must go without for the present. However, she thought she might get out and walk up and down for a few minutes to relieve the incipient cramp she could feel in her legs.

By dint of careful management, she contrived to get the door open. Then she uttered an exclamation. The river had risen to within four feet of where they were and, further away, she could see the water tearing along; she calculated that the dips must contain anything from five to eight feet. A fresh wind was blowing, and there was every indication that the weather of the day before was ended. As soon as they could get back to the fork, they would probably be able to find somewhere where they could make themselves fit to be seen, and then they must manage some sort of a meal.

She thought over their stores, and decided that it might be worse. At least everyone could have something to eat, and they could manage hot drinks with Jo's Etna. Bill took a final survey of conditions, and then turned back to the coach. Getting in was a much more delicate task than getting out had been, but the light was strengthening every minute, and she did it at last. Cornelia murmured something about "Horrid draught," so the mistress closed the door carefully, and returned to her suitcase, greatly refreshed. She took out her pocket comb, removed her hair pins, and proceeded to put her curly mop in order. A little cologne ice rubbed over her face and hands was the next thing; and then, feeling much better, she settled down to the last part of her watch.

It was an hour later when the men awoke. She heard them talking, and saw them leaving the cabin for a stroll round. Presently they returned and, a few minutes later, she felt the throbbing of the engine under her. She very much wondered if the girls would wake, but they were all far too tired to do so. Even when the coach began moving again they never stirred.

Miss Wilson sat on her case, drowsily wondering how long it would be before they could hope for a meal of some sort. She was longing for that hot drink! She glanced down at Miss Stewart and Joey, and wished she could sleep like that. It was the last thing she remembered doing. The next thing she knew, the girls, all very untidy and unwashed, with crumpled clothes and tousled heads, were sitting up in their places. The cases were neatly piled into the seats where they had been first put. Joey was busy balancing a biscuit tin on the Etna, which had been set in the lid of the same tin, and the coach was standing still on a high road which wound through a grassy valley where the sun, shining down on the rain-wet grass, made everything cheerful.

Bill started, and then rose with what dignity she could muster. "What time is it?" she asked.

"Seven o'clock," said Miss Stewart, looking up from her task of breaking up the chocolate collected the night before into the tin of steaming water.

"Good gracious! It was just four when I last looked at my watch!"

"Do you mean you stayed awake all that time?" asked Gillian in horror. "Oh, Miss Wilson!"

"Not quite all the time," replied Miss Wilson, shaking out her skirt. "I slept a little. But I didn't rest much until the last two or three hours. However did you people manage to put things straight without waking me?"

"Oh, that was me," said Joey with great lack of grammar, and most immodestly. "I woke up about six, and found that we were well away from our place of stranding, and the sun was shining. I got up, and Miss Stewart woke, too. We saw you were fast asleep, and I knew you hadn't been anywhere near it when we last chatted. Miss Stewart had roused about three, and seen you go out of the coach, so we gathered that you hadn't had much rest of any kind.

As the girls began to stir, we shut them up before they could speak, and I believe Miss Stewart promised history lines for every day left of the term to anyone who disturbed you. You *should* have seen the bee-yootiful way in which everyone moved about after that. As the girls got up, we made them stand in the aisle while I moved the cases and folded the rugs. Quite simple, you see!"

"Well, thank you very much," said Bill. "I feel better after that long nap. And now, I suppose, we have some sort of meal. Where are the men, Miss Stewart?"

"Gone to seek petrol," said Miss Stewart. "There, Joey, that's done, I think. How are we to lift it off?"

"Scarves, of course," said Joey. "Toss me a couple, someone!"

Cornelia and Evadne brought scarves, and the brimful tin was lifted to the floor, and then Jo turned herself into a minor whirlwind in an attempt to blow out the flames.

"Put the lid on," advised Miss Wilson.

"Can't!"

"Why not?"

"Because unfortunately, it got dropped into the brew and, as it was nearly boiling, and we hadn't any spoons, we couldn't get it out."

"Jo! What *will* the stuff taste like?"

"Mercifully, I boiled the whole thing after I'd used it last time, because something got spilt on it, so I don't believe it'll taste at all." Jo gave a final puff which nearly winded her, and the Etna went out in a flurry. "There you are! Now bring your mugs, ladies, and you shall have a nice drink!"

It was impossible to pour from the tin, so they had to dip their cups in. However, there was plenty of sugar, and it was hot, if it did have a queer flavour. Jo rescued the lid of her Etna when the last drops had been poured out, and then the girls settled down to a scratch meal of the remains of yesterday's supplies, the biscuits out of the tin, and some apples Louise had with her.

By the time it was over, the men had returned with a can of petrol, and presently they were once more on their way. They met with no further mishaps, and duly sailed up to the gates of the Chalet School somewhere about four o'clock that afternoon.

Thanks to a Gasthaus they had passed, where the hostess offered them all hot baths with much pride, they were clean, if somewhat rumpled about the clothes. Some of them were yawning, and Miss Wilson was very heavy about the eyes; but all in all, no one would have thought, to look at them, that they had had such an adventurous journey.

"I guessed you would be all right, and had only been held up by the storm," said Miss Annersley placidly when her colleagues went to report to her in the study. "It was awful at the Sonnalpe, and I imagine you caught it as badly if not worse."

"It wasn't exactly pleasant," said Miss Stewart, seeing that Miss Wilson was too busy suppressing yawns to be able to answer.

"I hope you found a nice Gasthaus for the night, and had comfortable beds?"

Bill stared wildly at her. Then she suddenly saw the funny side of it, and burst into shrieks of laughter. To think that, after all they had gone through, they should be greeted in this calm way! She caught Miss Stewart's eye, and the pair of them simply doubled up.

"What on earth is the joke?" demanded Miss Annersley suspiciously. "What have you people been doing?"

It was some time before they could sober down sufficiently to tell her, but when they did, their tale lost nothing in the telling. She listened to it with growing horror, especially when Miss Wilson told how she had got out of the coach in the early morning, and found the water nearly up to their wheels.

"Where is Joey?" she asked, when at length they had finished, and she had sympathized with them.

"Gone home to bed," said Miss Stewart. "We dropped her at Seespitz, and she said we were to tell you that not the King of England, the Pope, and Hitler all combined would get her out of it again before tomorrow morning."

"I'm going bedwards myself," said Bill with a fearful yawn. "Hilda, you'll excuse me, won't you? All I want is some hot milk, and then I'm going to sleep the clock round and more. I can scarcely keep my eyes open."

"Go to bed? I should think you *are* going to bed!" declared Matey, who had come into the room in time to hear most of the story. "Off with you to your room, and stay there till I've seen you tomorrow! You, too, Miss Stewart! Oh, I dare say you slept all right; but you look like an underdone suet pudding just now. And every one of the girls is going to do the same thing. I want to see and hear none of you till tomorrow. Now march – both of you!"

The two mistresses meekly marched. As Miss Stewart said next day, when Matey spoke like that the biggest autocrat on earth would have obeyed her. Besides, they were really very glad to get into pyjamas and snuggle down between the sheets with proper pillows under their heads.

No one took any harm from the adventure, though Madge Russell was horrified when she heard of it, and Dr Jem made all concerned take things easy for a day or two.

The final word came from Bill. "I told you you were boasting too soon," she informed the indignant Miss Stewart before the entire common room. 'Another time, perhaps, you'll believe me when I say that until our girls are safely under the roof of the school there's no possible means of telling what episodes one may meet. Stop giggling, all of you! I've a number of white hairs today that I didn't have before we went to Salzburg!"

CHAPTER 8

One at Last

"Now, Louise, have you got everything?"

"Yes, I think so, Matron. You'll come down presently and see that the Juniors and the nurses look all right, won't you?"

Matron nodded. "Oh, I'll come! Mind you see that all safety pins are properly fastened, and that the caps are on straight. Some of those children have no idea of wearing anything correctly."

Louise laughed, and then turned with her armful, and sped off downstairs.

It was the last day but one of term, and the annual garden party with which the summer term always closed was in preparation. They generally entertained their guests with some performance, and this year it had been decided to make a Guide affair of it. The Rangers would see to Kaffee und Kuchen, and the Cadets were to have a couple of stalls in aid of the free beds at the Sonnalpe which the school had maintained ever since the opening of the Sanatorium. The Brownies were to give a display, and it had been decided that they should present the story of Grace Darling, which would bring in a good deal of their Brownie work such as semaphore signalling, knot-tying, simple bandaging, laying tables, and making beds, while little Marie Varick, whose ambition it was to be an elocutionist some day, would tell the story first so that the continentals should know what it was all about.

The Guides were more ambitious. They were to represent hospital work in war time, and would show stretcher and first aid drill; sick nursing – including making of beds with patients in them; invalid cookery; tying of knots for nooses and lowering work; interpreting; short-hand and typewriting and book-keeping, since, as Bill had pointed out, to run a hospital you must understand the financial side as well as others; and, finally, tent-pitching. The nurses were to wear real nurses' uniform, and the four Matrons had been cajoled into lending sufficient "angel's-wing" caps for the occasion. Already in one of the big marquees beds had been set up for the "hospital"; and another held writing-desk, typewriter, telephone, and all the rest of the business paraphernalia.

Two performances were to be given, one in the afternoon, and one immediately after Kaffee und Kuchen, and the Brownies would do the same. This would mean that everyone would have a chance of seeing both shows.

As for the few unfortunates who, for one reason or another, were not members of the movements, they would act as hostesses. There *were* only a few of them, for the school ran three large Guide Companies, as well as the Ranger and Cadet Companies, and all the Juniors were Brownies.

Louise ran downstairs with her arms full of the great squares of cambric, and down the long corridors till she came to Hall, which had been built at a little distance from the school proper, and was joined to it by these light-wood passageways.

When she reached the building, she found Joey there in her new capacity of Lieutenant to the Tiernsee Third. Miss Anderson, who had held the post before, had been transferred to the Second to take the place of the former maths mistress, Miss Leslie, who had left at Easter to be married, so Jo had been called on to fill the breach, since she had been a keen Guide and an even keener Cadet. Although she had held the position for nearly six weeks now, she was still rather new to the work, and felt very self-conscious in her Guide's uniform.

"You do look professional, Jo!" said Louise as she laid

down her burden on the table with due regard for any creases.

Jo laughed and went pink. "I feel frightfully conspicuous," she confessed. Then she held out a square parcel. "Here's something for the library. It just came this morning, and I thought you people would like to have it to look at before you went off tomorrow – especially as some of you won't be coming back next term," she added with a rueful laugh.

"Jo! You don't mean it's *Cecily Holds the Fort*!"

It was as well, perhaps, that Louise had already laid down those caps, for she would certainly have dropped them anywhere in the excitement of the moment. Joey had always meant to be a writer when she grew up, and last autumn she had set to work and written a school story which had been lucky enough to take the fancy of the publishing firm to which she had sent it. She had had the proofs early in the spring, but no one had expected to see the completed book before the autumn. However, here it was, with Jo looking very shy for once in her life. What a thrill for the school!

"We must exhibit it, of course," began Louise as she started to undo the knot.

Joey swooped down on her and snatched the parcel from her fingers. "Oh, *no*, you don't! I very nearly didn't bring it because I thought you might try to do something mad like that. You'll promise me you'll just look at it, and then shove it away somewhere till this show is over, or I'll give it to my sister, and you won't get it till next term – which won't interest you, as you won't be here."

In vain Louise coaxed and stormed. Jo was determined. And then, just as the Head Girl had reluctantly given her word of honour that the book should not be exhibited, there came a clatter of feet, and the others poured in, all excited, and all talking at once.

Jo rose to the occasion. Blowing the "Freeze!" on her

whistle, she waited till they were all silent, and then bade them go quietly to the far wall and wait there while Louise told them what message Matey had sent. Then she turned to Louise who was still fondling the precious parcel.

"Your witness, sir!" she said lightly.

Louise nodded. Laying the book, still in its wrappings, on the table behind her, she said, "You are to get ready at once, and with as little noise and scrimmaging as possible. Matron is coming to examine everyone soon, and you are all to be ready for her when she comes. Get into your uniforms, and those who are to be nurses come to me to have your caps fixed as soon as you are ready. Jo and I will do them."

"Well, I like that!" gasped Jo as the others set to work to change. "Who said I was going to help?"

"Then what are you a Lieutenant for?" demanded Louise.

Joey laughed, and went to the help of Polly Heriot, who was struggling with her thick, long hair, and Louise, picking up the parcel once more, strolled over to a distant window to examine its contents. She was joined there by Hilary, who had brought an armful of signalling-flags for Anne, who was responsible for the signalling, to look over.

"Someone would get into trouble over rolling up her flag like a duster if there was time," she observed. "Hello! What's that? Is it your birthday, by any chance?"

'No, not till next month. This is much more important," said Louise, as she finally undid the knot and tore off the paper. "Look here, Hilary!"

A wail from Anne, who had come in and was examining her flags, passed unnoticed by either of them as they eagerly examined the precious book. Such an attractive dust jacket with a picture of a jolly schoolgirl bearing aloft a standard! Beneath this was a bright blue back, and there were four charming illustrations, the frontispiece being coloured. The two big girls peeped here and there in the book, and were thrilled with it.

"I'm going to get a copy, of course," said Louise. "I'll get Jo to autograph it for me. Oh, just fancy having a real live writer belonging to us!"

"Yes, it makes *me* feel a bit peacocky," acknowledged Hilary. "I'll get a copy, too, and then I can show it to people and say that the writer was Head Girl of my school only a year ago! Swish!"

Louise glanced at her in startled fashion, but had no time to say anything, since Joyce Linton was coming to have her cap arranged. Hurriedly she passed the book to Hilary. "Here! Hide it somewhere! I promised Jo we'd say nothing about it till the party is over. Put it behind Thomas More. No one is likely to see it there."

"All right," laughed Hilary. "He ought to take care of it, since he was a writer himself."

Louise went to attend to Joyce, and Hilary reached up and tucked the book behind the statue of the great Chancellor, which stood in Hall because, as well as being a great saint and a great man, he had been one of the first men to insist that his girls should be as well educated as his one boy.

After that, everyone was extremely busy – especially Anne, who, vowing vengeance on some careless persons, had brought the electric iron and plugged it in, and was busy ironing morse-flags which looked as if they had indeed been used as dusters. Matron arrived in the midst of all this, and inspected the "nurses". Louise and Jo had done their work well, and there was no fault to find. The young nurses looked very attractive in their uniforms, with the flowing lines of the caps round their young faces. Joyce Linton especially looked lovely, though no one informed her of the fact. Miss Joyce was not ignorant of her good looks, and no one wanted to make her conceited.

"Just keep those caps as they are," said Matron finally, "and try not to crumple them more than necessary. Kitty Burnett, if you finger your apron like that it will be a rag before ever you have to appear in it. Marie Varick, come here and let me pull that jersey of yours straight. Now then; if you're all ready, you'd best get to your posts. Anne, what *is* the awful smell of turpentine?''

"It's me," confessed Anne, looking up from her last flag. 'Otto has been doing some touching-up on the paintwork, and I wiped off about half a yard of white paint with my skirt. Luckily he had turps handy, and he gave it to me before tearing off to see what damage I'd done to his priceless posts.''

"Where have you put what was left of it?'' demanded Matron.

"Over there in the corner by the window. I'll take it back to the shed when I go; but I met Hilary, and she called out that some of the flags looked like dish cloths, so I rushed here to see to it. Whoever had them last ought to be shot!''

"I dare say! Mind you don't forget to take that stuff away. And don't forget to switch off the iron, either. We don't want the electricity wasted, you know.''

Matron rustled off, very fresh and neat in her stiffly-starched uniform, and Anne bent her energies to finishing the ironing of the flags. She had finished and was just rolling them up when Polly Heriot, who had left Hall ten minutes previously, appeared followed by someone Anne had not expected to see. The day before, she had had a letter from her mother, who was up at the Sonnalpe with Anne's youngest aunt. The letter had told her that Aunt Lucia was very ill, and Mrs Seymour did not think she could come to the garden party. And here she was! With a cry of joy, Anne dumped down the iron on the table, and sprang to greet her, and then went off with her, chattering happily.

Anne had only twenty minutes with her mother before she was called away to attend to her own particular job, and after that the afternoon was so full that no one had time for anything but the immediate business in hand.

It was nearly five o'clock when Betty Wynne-Davies, who was with Mrs Russell and consequently on her best behaviour, suddenly said in puzzled tones, "Madame! What is that funny mist behind the trees?"

Mrs Russell and the Robin, who was there too, turned in the direction in which Betty was pointing. Sure enough, there was a thin, bluish mist rising, and getting thicker every minute.

"It's fire!" cried Madge Russell. "Something has set Hall on fire! Run, Betty! Find some of the prefects and send them to me there. Robin, you go and seek Uncle Jem, and tell him. Don't go near Hall!" Then, only waiting to watch both little girls speeding off, she caught up her pretty, rose-spattered skirt, and raced lightly as any schoolgirl for the spot.

When she got there, Mrs Russell gave an involuntary cry of horror. From the windows at one end of the building came not only smoke, but tongues of fire; and already they seemed to be spreading. The building was lined with asbestos; but outside it was wood and plaster, like most buildings in the Tiernthal. Unless something was done at once, the whole place must be doomed.

Then she glanced along. The passageway was not even asbestos-lined; if it caught, it would blaze like tinder, for they had had very little rain for the past three weeks, and everything was as dry as could be. If the passageway caught, it was likely that the Chalet itself would go. That must be prevented at all costs! The passageway must come down!

Even as the thought came, the pealing of the great alarm bell in the turret at Ste Thérèse's told her that help was at hand, and almost at once there came the sound of hasty footsteps, and half a dozen people, followed by Otto and his satellites, burst through the bushes, dragging with them the huge school hose.

"The passageway!" cried Madge. "Leave the hose to someone else, Otto, and go and get axes – spades – anything that will smash! It must come down at once!"

Jem, who had just arrived, snatched the hose from Otto's hands, and aided by the school fire brigade, who backed him up nobly, directed the mouth at the burning wood. Otto tore off, and presently the sound of heavy implements on wood and sundry crashes told the young owner of the school that the work of destruction was being carried out.

Meanwhile, some had rushed down to the lake to help with the pump, and already a powerful jet of water was being played on the burning wood. A lighter hose had been brought from a nearby hotel, and this was used on that part of Hall which had not yet been fired; while buckets of water were being passed from hand to hand up the two long chains which the Guides had formed, and were dashed by members of the staff against the flames, which seemed likely to give way before the furious onslaught.

Suddenly, there broke a cry from Louise, "Joey's book! We left it in Hall! It'll be burnt to ashes!" Breaking away, she made a dash for the nearest doorway, and pushed hard. It swung open, and a great cloud of smoke rolled out. Before anyone could stop her, she had struggled in; and, as a matter of fact, only three people did see her go. One was Gillian Linton, who was helping with the hose, and therefore could do nothing; the second was Jockel, the poor, half-witted lad who did some of the rough work; the third was Hilary, who was helping to beat out any smouldering grass round Hall, and who guessed at once what had happened.

Dropping her bough, she sprang after Louise, and nearly staggered back as she caught the full volume of smoke. But she remembered what she had been taught at Rangers and, snatching out her handkerchief, held it over nose and mouth. Then, with eyes already smarting and watering, she dropped onto all fours, and crawled in to seek Louise.

It was a terribly long business – or so it seemed to her; but suddenly, just as she was about to give up, she put her hand on woollen material, and realized that it was a Guide skirt. Gripping firmly with her free hand, she felt up till she got to the shoulders. Then, dropping all precautions, she put her hands under them, got to her feet and tugged with all her might.

After all, she was only just inside the doorway. She had wasted time in looking for her friend in the smother of smoke. Just as Bill and Miss Annersley, sent there by Gillian's cry of "Louise has gone into Hall!" arrived, frantic with worry, she staggered out, dragging a white and half-suffocated Louise with her. She stumbled into Miss Annersley, lost her balance, and fell headlong on top of Miss Wilson.

Mercifully, no harm had been done. Louise was half-stifled with all the smoke she had swallowed, and her uniform was ruined; while Hilary was black with soot, and her eyes were red-rimmed and sore. But that was all. As for Hall, thanks to the prompt measures taken, not much damage was done there, though the passageway would have to be built up again. Two window frames had disappeared, and part of the outside was gone, too. But, thanks to the asbestos lining, the interior was fairly whole. The big trestle-table which had held their gadgets was lying in a heap of ashes on the floor; but the other which had held the school's clothes was uninjured. The frocks would wash, and the building itself could be cleaned and repainted in a few weeks. Even Thomas More would only need a good scrubbing to put him right. And Jo's precious book was safe, thought the jacket had lost its pristine freshness.

As to how the fire had occurred, that was easily decided when a queer-looking contraption came to light among the ruins of the table. In her excitement at seeing her mother, Anne had forgotten to switch off the iron. She had not even up-ended it. The result was that by degrees the heat had scorched through the ironing blankets and sheets, which had first smouldered and then burst into flame. The flames had reached Otto's turpentine can – providentially, Anne had used most of it on her skirt, and there had been a bare teaspoonful in it – and the result had been a flare-up which had caught the wooden framework of the window. The fire had followed.

Anne was nearly heartbroken over it. She was so upset that no one had the heart to say much to her. "I risked my own life and Joey's last summer for a silly freak in the Flower valley," she told Madge Russell, who came to reassure her. "This summer, I've nearly burnt the school to the ground through my own abominable carelessness. Oh, Madame! Can you ever forgive me?"

"Easily," said Madge in her most matter-of-fact tones. "Don't be silly, Anne. It was stupid to leave the iron flat on the board. If it had been on end nothing would have happened. But it was an accident. Louise has only herself to thank for her share in the business; and the same applies to Hilary. So pull yourself together, Anne, and don't be so selfish as to make yourself ill with fretting over what can't be helped now. Only do, for pity's sake, learn to switch off the electricity in the future!"

This very calm and sane way of taking what had seemed to her no less than a tragedy helped to make Anne see things in a less morbid light; and by the time the summer was ended, she was herself.

As for Louise, she received a very severe rebuke from Miss Annersley, who pointed out that she had no right to risk her life for a mere three-and-sixpenny book which could – and would – have been replaced next day. Louise, who was dreadfully ashamed of having lost her head as she did, was very penitent, and vowed that she would make every effort to learn self control. She knew quite well that she should have let the book go. Perhaps the general excitement of the garden party had helped to upset her usual equilibrium.

Even Hilary came in for her share, for, as Miss Annersley told her plainly, her business was to call someone in authority, and not risk her life that way.

"No hope of being let feel that we are heroines," grumbled Hilary with mock discontent to Gillian after it was all over. "Oh, the Abbess is right, and I know it – and if I can pull your leg like that, you ought to be in the Kinder!"

Gillian laughed. "Never mind, Hilary! Whatever the staff may say, the school thinks you a real heroine. When you are Head Girl here—"

"Yes, when!" scoffed Hilary. "I've only another year, and you know that you're to be Head Girl, so what chance have I?"

"I'm leaving at Christmas," returned Gillian quietly. "I shall be almost eighteen then, and Mummy needs me. You're practically safe to be Head Girl after me. Such crowds are leaving this term – Lulu, Paula, Margia, Luigia, Anne, Arda, Cyrilla, and Elsie – that we'll be a good deal alone in our glory. Ida and Nancy are leaving next term, too, they tell me; and Madame and the Abbess won't see having Lonny Barkocz for Head when she's been in Upper Sixth only one term. Her turn will come next September; she's not quite sixteen, even now. So you're pretty safe for it, I think."

Hilary went scarlet, and her blue eyes were filled with longing. 'I wish I could believe you!"

"Why, wouldn't you have been Head Girl at St Scholastika's if that had carried on?"

"There *was* a rumour to that effect," admitted Hilary.

"Very well, then. It's only been put off for two terms. Oh yes, Hilary! You've missed being Head Girl of the Saints; but you may prepare to be Head Girl of the Chalet!"

"Quite right," said Jo's voice behind them. "It'll be rather fun for you, Hilary, for the new House arrangements will have settled down by then, and got into working order. Oh, I do wish I might be here to share in it all!"

"Get Dr Jem to bring you all down to the lake for the skating, then," suggested Gillian, while Hilary exclaimed with surprise. "Peggy and Rix will be old enough to learn by then, and Bride and David and Primula Mary can be hauled about the chairs. It would be fun, Jo!"

"It would," agreed Joey. "I must see what can be done about it."

"Still, it won't be the same as having you at school," sighed Hilary; "but if you're just at the other side of the lake, Jo, I can come across for advice and help when I need it – *if* I need it. You may both be quite wrong, you know," she added.

"We're not," said Gillian. "I'm going to get you to help me in all sorts of ways next term, so that you'll be in the way of things, and can slip into my place easily."

Hilary flushed again. "You know," she said slowly, "I didn't *want* to be Head of Scholastika's in the least. I felt far too young and kiddish. But if you two *are* right, and if I'm really Head Girl here after Christmas, I shall simply love it. It seems, somehow, such a big honour!"

"Well, so it is," said Gillian. She slipped her hand through Hilary's arm chummily. "After all, Hilary, it isn't just being Head of the Chalet *or* Scholastika's, but being Head of *both*."

"No," said Jo gravely. "It isn't that either – it's more."

"Of course," said Hilary, her face suddenly lighting up. "It's being Head of the biggest Chalet School there's ever been. For you know, Gill and Jo, we may have felt divided at the beginning of term, but now we aren't two schools at all – we're *one*!"

Jo nodded. "That's true – one school – the *new* Chalet School!"